"What did you wish?" Quinn asked,
a gruff note to his voice.

Tess made a face. "If I tell you, it won't come true. Don't you know anything about wishes?"

Right now, he could tell her a thing or two about wanting something he shouldn't. That sensuous heat wrapped tighter around his insides. "I know enough. For instance, I know sometimes wishes can be completely ridiculous and make no sense. For instance, right now, I wish I could kiss you. Don't ask me why. I don't even like you."

Her eyes looked huge and green in her delicate face as she stared at him. "Okay," she said, her voice breathy.

"Okay, I can kiss you? Or, okay, you won't ask why I want to?"

She let out a ragged-sounding breath. "Either. Both."

He didn't need much more of an invitation than that. Without allowing himself to stop and think, he stepped forward and covered her mouth with his.

Dear Reader,

It is with great delight that I introduce another trilogy as part of my loosely connected THE COWBOYS OF COLD CREEK series. When I wrote the first books in the series, I never expected so many other ideas to keep flying about others in the fictional community of Pine Gulch, Idaho. It's been wonderful to revisit old friends!

A Cold Creek Homecoming kicks off the miniseries about four people with troubled childhoods who were taken in by a ranching couple as foster children. I loved writing the stories of Quinn Southerland and Tess Claybourne and helping them sort through their tangled past to find happiness. And I'm very much looking forward to writing about Quinn's foster siblings, Brant Western, Cisco Del Norte and Easton Springhill.

All my best,

RaeAnne

A COLD CREEK HOMECOMING

RAEANNE THAYNE

Silhouette

SPECIAL EDITION

Published by Silhouette Books

America's Publisher of Contemporary Romance

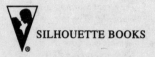

SILHOUETTE BOOKS

ISBN-13: 978-0-373-65478-9

A COLD CREEK HOMECOMING

Recycling programs
for this product may
not exist in your area.

Visit Silhouette Books at www.eHarlequin.com

Printed in U.S.A.

Books by RaeAnne Thayne

RAEANNE THAYNE

finds inspiration in the beautiful northern Utah mountains, where she lives with her husband and three children. Her books have won numerous honors, including three RITA® Award nominations from Romance Writers of America and a Career Achievement Award from *Romantic Times BOOKreviews* magazine. RaeAnne loves to hear from readers and can be reached through her Web site at www.raeannethayne.com.

In memory of my dear aunt, Arlene Wood,
for afghans and parachutes and ceramic frogs.
I only wish I'd dedicated one to you before!
And to Jennifer Black, my sister and hero,
for helping her pass with peace and dignity.

Chapter One

"You're home!"

The thin, reedy voice whispering from the frail woman on the bed was nothing like Quinn Southerland remembered.

Though she was small in stature, Jo Winder's voice had always been firm and commanding, just like the rest of her personality. When she used to call them in for supper, he and the others could hear her voice ringing out loud and clear from one end of the ranch to the other. No matter where they were, they knew the moment they heard that voice, it was time to go back to the house.

Now the woman who had done so much to raise him—the toughest woman he had ever known—seemed a tiny, withered husk of herself, her skin papery and pale and her voice barely audible.

The cracks in his heart from watching her endure the long months and years of her illness widened a little more. To his great shame, he had a sudden impulse to run away, to escape back to Seattle and his business and the comfortable life he had created for himself there, where he could pretend this was all some kind of bad dream and she was immortal, as he had always imagined.

Instead, he forced himself to step forward to the edge of the bed, where he carefully folded her bony fingers in his own much larger ones, cursing the cancer that was taking away this woman he loved so dearly.

He gave her his most charming smile, the one that never failed to sway any woman in his path, whether in the boardroom or the bedroom.

"Where else would I be but right here, darling?"

The smile she offered in return was rueful and she lifted their entwined fingers to her cheek. "You shouldn't have come. You're so busy in Seattle."

"Never too busy for my best girl."

Her laugh was small but wryly amused, as it always used to be when he would try to charm his way out of trouble with her.

Jo wasn't the sort who could be easily charmed but she never failed to appreciate the effort.

"I'm sorry to drag you down here," she said. "I…only wanted to see all of my boys one last time."

He wanted to protest that his foster mother would be around for years to come, that she was too tough and ornery to let a little thing like cancer stop her, but he couldn't deny the evidence in front of him.

She was dying, was much closer to it than any of them had feared.

"I'm here, as long as you need me," he vowed.

"You're a good boy, Quinn. You always have been."

He snorted at that—both of them knew better about that, as well. "Easton didn't tell me you've been hitting the weed as part of your treatment."

The blankets rustled softly as her laugh shook her slight frame. "You know better than that. No marijuana here."

"Then what are you smoking?"

"Nothing. I meant what I said. You were always a good boy on the inside, even when you were dragging the others into trouble."

"It still means the world that you thought so." He kissed her forehead. "Now I can see you're tired. You get some rest and we can catch up later."

"I would give anything for just a little of my old energy."

Her voice trailed off on the last word and he could tell she had already drifted off, just like that, in mid-sentence. As he stood beside her bed, still holding her fingers, she winced twice in her sleep.

He frowned, hating the idea of her hurting. He slowly, carefully, released her fingers as if they would shatter at his touch and laid them with gentle care on the bed then turned just as Easton Springhill, his distant cousin by marriage and the closest thing he had to a sister, appeared in the doorway of the bedroom.

He moved away from the bed and followed Easton outside the room.

"She seems in pain," he said, his voice low with distress.

"She is," Easton answered. "She doesn't say much about it but I can tell it's worse the past week or so."

"Isn't there something we can do?"

"We have a few options. None of them last very long. The hospice nurse should be here any minute. She can give her something for the pain." She tilted her head. "When was the last time you ate?"

He tried to remember. He had been in Tokyo when he got the message from Easton that Jo was asking for him to come home. Though he had had two more days of meetings scheduled for a new shipping route he was negotiating, he knew he had no choice but to drop everything. Jo would never have asked if the situation hadn't been dire.

So he had rescheduled everything and ordered his plane back to Pine Gulch. Counting several flight delays from bad weather over the Pacific, he had been traveling for nearly eighteen hours and had been awake for eighteen before that.

"I had something on the plane, but it's been a few hours."

"Let me make you a sandwich, then you can catch a few z's."

"You don't have to wait on me." He followed her down the long hall and into the cheery white-and-red kitchen. "You've got enough to do, running the ranch and taking care of Jo. I've been making my own sandwiches for a long time now."

"Don't you have people who do that for you?"

"Sometimes," he admitted. "That doesn't mean I've forgotten how."

"Sit down," she ordered him. "I know where everything is here."

He thought about pushing her. But lovely as she was with her delicate features and long sweep of blond hair,

Easton could be as stubborn and ornery as Jo and he was just too damn tired for another battle.

Instead, he eased into one of the scarred pine chairs snugged up against the old table and let her fuss over him for a few moments. "Why didn't you tell me how things were, East? She's withered away in the three months since I've been home. Chester probably weighs more than she does."

At the sound of his name, Easton's retired old cow dog that followed her or Jo everywhere lifted his grizzled gray muzzle and thumped his black-and-white tail against the floor.

Easton's sigh held exhaustion and discouragement and no small measure of guilt. "I wanted to. I swear. I threatened to call you all back weeks ago but she begged me not to say anything. She said she didn't want you to know how things were until…"

Her voice trailed off and her mouth trembled a little. He didn't need her to finish. Jo wouldn't have wanted them to know until close to the end.

This was it. For three long years, Jo had been fighting breast cancer and now it seemed her battle was almost over.

He *hated* this. He wanted to escape back to his own world where he could at least pretend he had some semblance of control. But she wanted him here in Cold Creek, so here he would damn well stay.

"Truth time, East. How long does she have?"

Easton's features tightened with a deep sorrow. She had lost so much, this girl he had thought of as a sister since the day he arrived at Winder Ranch two decades ago, an angry, bitter fourteen-year-old with nothing but attitude. Easton had lived in the foreman's house then with her parents and they had been friends almost from the moment he arrived.

"Three weeks or so," she said. "Maybe less. Maybe a little more."

He wanted to rant at the unfairness of it all that somebody like Jo would be taken from the earth with such cruelty when she had spent just about every moment of her entire seventy-two years of life giving back to others.

"I'll stay until then."

She stared at him, the butter knife she was using to spread mustard on his sandwich frozen in her hand. "How can you possibly be away from Southerland Shipping that long?"

He shrugged. "I might need to make a few short trips back to Seattle here and there but most of my work can be done long-distance through e-mail and conference calls. It shouldn't be a problem. And I have good people working for me who can handle most of the complications that might come up."

"That's not what she wanted when she asked you to come home one more time," Easton protested.

"Maybe not. But she isn't making the decisions about this, as much as she might think she's the one in charge. This is what I want. I should have come home when things first starting spiraling down. It wasn't fair for us to leave her care completely in your hands."

"You didn't know how bad things were."

If he had visited more, he would have seen for himself. But like Brant and Cisco, the other two foster sons Jo and her husband, Guff, had made a home for, life had taken him away from the safety and peace he had always found at Winder Ranch.

"I'm staying," he said firmly. "I can certainly spare a few weeks to help you out on the ranch and with Jo's care and whatever else you need, after all she and Guff did for me. Don't argue with me on this, because you won't win."

"I wasn't going to argue," she said. "You can't know how happy she'll be to have you here. Thank you, Quinn."

The relief in her eyes told him with stark clarity how difficult it must have been for Easton to watch Jo dying, especially after she had lost her own parents at a young age and then her beloved uncle who had taken her in after their deaths.

He squeezed her fingers when she handed him a sandwich with thick slices of homemade bread and hearty roast beef. "Thanks. This looks delicious."

She slid across from him with an apple and a glass of milk. As he looked at her slim wrists curved around her glass, he worried that, like Jo, she hadn't been eating enough and was withering away.

"What about the others?" he asked, after one fantastic bite. "Have you let Brant and Cisco know how things stand?"

Jo had always called them her Four Winds, the three foster boys she and Guff had taken in and Easton, her niece who had been their little shadow.

"We talk to Brant over the computer every couple weeks when he can call us from Afghanistan. Our Web cam's not the greatest but I suppose he still had front-row seats as her condition has deteriorated over the past month. He's working on swinging leave and is trying to get here as soon as he can."

Quinn winced as guilt pinched at him. His best friend was halfway around the world and had done a better job of keeping track of things here at the ranch than Quinn had when he was only a few states away.

"What about Cisco?"

She looked down at her apple. "Have you heard from him?"

"No. Not for a while. I got a vague e-mail in the spring but nothing since."

"Neither had we. It's been months. I've tried everything I can think of to reach him but I have no idea even where he is. Last I heard, he was in El Salvador or somewhere like that but I'm not having any luck turning up any information about him."

Cisco worried him, Quinn had to admit. The rest of them had gone on to do something productive with their lives. Quinn had started Southerland Shipping after a stint in the Air Force, Brant Western was an honorable Army officer serving his third tour of duty in the Middle East and Easton had the ranch, which she loved more than just about anything.

Cisco Del Norte, on the other hand, had taken a very different turn. Quinn had only seen him a few times in the past five or six years and he seemed more and more jaded as the years passed.

What started as a quick trip to Mexico to visit relatives after a stint in the Army had turned into years of Cisco bouncing around Central and South America.

Quinn had no idea what he did down there. He suspected that few of Cisco's activities were legal and none of them were good. He had decided several years ago that he was probably better off not knowing for sure.

But he *did* know Jo would want one more chance to see Cisco, whatever he was up to south of the border.

He swallowed another bite of sandwich. "I'll put some resources on it and see what I can find out. My assistant is frighteningly efficient. If anyone can find the man and drag him out of whatever cantina he calls home these days, it's Kathleen."

Easton's smile didn't quite reach her eyes. "I've met the redoubtable Kathleen. She scares me."

"That makes two of us. It's all part of her charm."

He tried to hide his sudden jaw-popping yawn behind a sip of water, but few things slipped past Easton.

"Get some sleep," she ordered in a tone that didn't leave room for arguments. "Your old room is ready for you. Clean sheets and everything."

"I don't need to sleep. I'll stay up with Jo."

"I've got it. She's got my cell on speed dial and only has to hit a couple of buttons to reach me all the time. Besides, the hospice nurse will be here to take care of things during the night."

"That's good. I was about to ask what sort of medical care she receives."

"Every three hours, we have a home-care nurse check in to adjust medication and take care of any other needs she might have. Jo doesn't think it's necessary to have that level of care, but it's what her doctors and I think is best."

That relieved his mind considerably. At least Easton didn't have to carry every burden by herself. He rose from the table and folded her into a hug.

"I'm glad you're here," she murmured. "It helps."

"This is where I have to be. Wake me up if you or Jo need anything."

"Right."

He headed up the stairs in the old log house, noting the fourth step from the top still creaked, just like always. He had hated that step. More than once it had been the architect of his downfall when he and one of the others tried to sneak in after curfew. They would always try so hard to be quiet but then that blasted stair would always give them away. By the time they would reach the top of the staircase, there would be Guff, waiting for them with those bushy white eyebrows raised and a judgment-day look on his features.

He almost expected to see his foster father waiting for him on the landing. Instead, only memories hovered there as he pushed open his bedroom door, remembering how suspicious and belligerent he had been to the Winders when he first arrived.

He had viewed Winder Ranch as just another prison, one more stop on the misery train that had become his life after his parents' murder-suicide.

Instead, he had found only love here.

Jo and Guff Winder had loved him. They had welcomed him into their home and their hearts, and then made more room for first Brant and then Cisco.

Their love hadn't stopped him from his share of trouble through high school but he knew that without them, he probably would have nurtured that bitterness and hate festering inside him and ended up in prison or dead by now.

This was where he needed to be. As long as Jo hung in, he would be here—for her and for Easton. It was the right thing—the *only* thing—to do.

* * *

He completely slept through the discreet alarm on his Patek Philippe, something he *never* did.

When he finally emerged from his exhausted slumber three hours later, Quinn was disoriented at first. The sight of his familiar bedroom ceiling left him wondering if he was stuck in some kind of weird flashback about his teenage years, the kind of dream where some sexy, tight-bodied cheerleader was going to skip through the door any minute now.

No. That wasn't it. Something bleak tapped at his memory bank and the cheerleader fantasy bounced back through the door.

Jo.

He was at the ranch and Jo was dying. He sat up and scrubbed at his face. Daylight was still several hours away but he was on Tokyo time and doubted he could go back to sleep anyway.

He needed a shower, but he supposed it could wait for a few more moments, until he checked on her. Since Jo had always expressed strongly negative feelings about the boys going shirtless around her ranch even when they were mowing the lawn, he took a moment to shrug back into his travel-wrinkled shirt and headed down the stairs, careful this time to skip over the noisy step so he didn't wake Easton.

When he was a kid, Jo and Guff had shared a big master suite on the second floor. She had moved out of it after Guff's death five years ago from an unexpected heart attack, saying she couldn't bear sleeping there anymore without him. She had taken one of the two bedrooms on the main floor, the one closest to the kitchen.

When he reached it, he saw a woman backing out of the room, closing the door quietly behind her.

For an instant, he assumed it was Easton, but then he saw the coloring was wrong. Easton wore her waterfall of straight honey-blond hair in a ponytail most of the time but this woman had short, wavy auburn hair that just passed her chin.

She was smaller than Easton, too, though definitely curvy in all the right places. He felt a little thrum of masculine interest at the sight of a delectably curved derriere easing from the room—as unexpected as it was out of place, under the circumstances.

He was just doing his best to tamp his inappropriate interest back down when the woman turned just enough that he could see her features and any fledgling attraction disappeared like he'd just jumped naked into Windy Lake.

"What the hell are you doing here?" he growled out of the darkness.

Chapter Two

The woman whirled and grabbed at her chest, her eyes wide in the dimly lit hallway. "My word! You scared the life out of me!"

Quinn considered himself a pretty easygoing guy and he had despised very few people in his life—his father came immediately to mind as an exception.

But if he had to make a list, Tess Jamison would be right there at the top.

He was about to ask her again what she thought she was doing creeping around Winder Ranch when his sleep-deprived synapses finally clicked in and he made the connection as he realized that curvy rear end he had been unknowingly admiring was encased in deep blue flowered surgical scrubs.

She carried a basket of medical supplies in one

hand and had an official-looking clipboard tucked under her arm.

"*You're* the hospice nurse?" His voice rose with incredulity.

She fingered the silver stethoscope around her neck with her free hand. "That's what they tell me. Hey, Quinn. How have you been?"

He must still be upstairs in his bed, having one of those infinitely disturbing dreams of high school, the kind where he shows up to an advanced placement class and discovers he hasn't read a single page of the textbook, knows absolutely none of the subject matter, and is expected to sit down and ace the final.

This couldn't be real. It was too bizarre, too surreal, that someone he hadn't seen since graduation night—and would have been quite content never to have to see again—would suddenly be standing in the hallway of Winder Ranch looking much the same as she had fifteen years earlier.

He blinked but, damn it all, she didn't disappear and he wished he could just wake up, already.

"Tess," he said gruffly, unable to think of another thing to say.

"Right."

"How long have you been coming here to take care of Jo?"

"Two weeks now," she answered, and he wondered if her voice had always had that husky note to it or if it was a new development. "There are several of us, actually. I usually handle the nights. I stop in about every three or four hours to check vitals and help Jo manage her pain.

I juggle four other patients with varying degrees of need but she's my favorite."

As she spoke, she moved away from Jo's bedroom door and headed toward him. He held his breath and fought the instinct to cover his groin, just as a precaution.

Not that she had ever physically hurt him in their turbulent past, but Tess Jamison—Homecoming Queen, valedictorian, and all-around Queen Bee, probably for Bitch—had a way of emasculating a man with just a look.

She smelled not like the sulfur and brimstone he might have expected, but a pleasant combination of vanilla and peaches that made him think of hot summer evenings out on the wide porch of the ranch with a bowl of ice cream and Jo's divine cobbler.

She headed down the hall toward the kitchen, where she flipped on a small light over the sink.

For the first time, he saw her in full light. She was as lovely as when she wore the Homecoming Queen crown, with high cheekbones, a delicate nose and the same lush, kissable mouth he remembered.

Her eyes were still her most striking feature, green and vivid, almond-shaped, with thick, dark lashes.

But fifteen years had passed and nothing stayed the same except his memories. She had lost that fresh-faced innocent look that had been so misleading. He saw tiny, faint lines fanning out at the edges of her eyes and she wore a bare minimum of makeup.

"I didn't know you were back," she finally said when he continued to stare. "Easton didn't mention it before she went to bed."

Apparently there were several things Easton was keeping close to her sneaky little vest. "I only arrived this evening." Somehow he managed to answer her without snarling, but it was a chore. "Jo wanted to see all of us one more time."

He couldn't quite bring himself to say *last* instead of *more* but those huge green eyes still softened.

She was a hospice nurse, he reminded himself, as tough as he found that to believe. She was probably well-trained to pretend sympathy. The real Tess Jamison didn't care about another soul on the planet except herself.

"Are you here for the weekend?" she asked.

"Longer," he answered, his voice curt. It was none of her business that he planned to stay at Winder Ranch as long as Jo needed him, which he hoped was much longer than the doctors seemed to believe.

She nodded once, her eyes solemn, and he knew she understood all he hadn't said. The soft compassion in those eyes—and his inexplicable urge to soak it in—turned him conversely hostile.

"I can't believe you've stuck around Pine Gulch all these years," he drawled. "I would have thought Tess Jamison couldn't wait to shake the dust of podunk eastern Idaho off her designer boots."

She smiled a little. "It's Tess Claybourne now. And plans have a way of changing, don't they?"

"I'm starting to figure that out."

Curiosity stirred inside him. What had she been doing the past fifteen years? Why that hint of sadness in her eyes?

This was Tess, he reminded himself. He didn't give a damn what she'd been up to, even if she looked hauntingly lovely in the low light of the kitchen.

"So you married old Scott, huh? What's he up to? All that quarterback muscle probably turned to flab, right? Is he ranching with his dad?"

She pressed her lips into a thin line for just a moment, then gave him another of those tiny smiles, this one little more than a taut stretch of her mouth. "None of those things, I'm afraid. He died almost two years ago."

Quinn gave an inward wince at his own tactlessness. Apparently nothing had changed. She had *always* brought out the worst in him.

"How?"

She didn't answer for a moment, instead crossing to the coffeemaker he had assumed Easton must have forgotten to turn off. Now he realized she must have left a fresh pot for the hospice worker, since Tess seemed completely comfortable reaching in the cabinet for a cup and pouring.

"Pneumonia," she finally answered as she added two packets of sweetener. "Scott died of pneumonia."

"Really?" That seemed odd. He thought only old people and little kids could get that sick from pneumonia.

"He was…ill for a long time before that. His immune system was compromised and he couldn't fight it off."

Quinn wasn't a *complete* ass, even when it came to this woman he despised so much. He forced himself to offer the appropriate condolences. "That must have been rough for you. Any kids?"

"No."

This time she didn't even bother to offer a tight smile, only stared into the murky liquid swirling in her cup and he thought again how surreal this was, standing in the

Winder Ranch kitchen in the middle of the night having a conversation with her, when he had to fight down every impulse to snarl and yell and order her out of the house.

"Jo tells me you run some big shipping company in the Pacific Northwest," she said after a moment.

"That's right." The third biggest in the region, but he was hoping that with the new batch of contracts he was negotiating Southerland Shipping would soon slide into the number two spot and move up from there.

"She's so proud of you boys and Easton. She talks about you all the time."

"Does she?" He wasn't at all thrilled to think about Jo sharing with Tess any details of his life.

"Oh, yes. I'm sure she's thrilled to have you home. That must be why she was sleeping so peacefully. She didn't even wake when I checked her vitals, which is unusual. Jo's usually a light sleeper."

"How are they?"

"Excuse me?"

"Her vitals. How is she?"

He hated to ask, especially of Tess, but he was a man who dealt best with challenges when he gathered as much information as possible.

She took another sip of coffee then poured the rest down the sink and turned on the water to wash it down.

"Her blood pressure is still lower than we'd like to see and she's needing oxygen more and more often. She tries to hide it but she's in pain most of the time. I'm sorry. I wish I had something better to offer you."

"It's not your fault," he said, even as he wished he could somehow figure out a way to blame her for it.

"That's funny. It feels that way sometimes. It's my

job to make her as comfortable as possible but she doesn't want to spend her last days in a drugged haze, she says. So we're limited in some of our options. But we still do our best."

He couldn't imagine *anyone* deliberately choosing this for a career. Why on earth would a woman like Tess Jamison—Claybourne now, he reminded himself—have chosen to stick around tiny Pine Gulch and become a hospice nurse? He couldn't quite get past the incongruity of it.

"I'd better go," she said. "I've got three more patients to check on tonight. I'll be back in a few hours, though, and Easton knows she can call me anytime if she needs me. It's…good to see you again, Quinn."

He wouldn't have believed her words, even if he didn't see the lie in her vivid green eyes. She wasn't any happier to see him than he had been to find her wandering the halls of Winder Ranch.

Still, courtesy drilled into him by Jo demanded he walk her to the door. He stood on the porch and watched through the darkness until she reached her car, then he walked back inside, shaking his head.

Tess Jamison Claybourne.

As if he needed one more miserable thing to face here in Pine Gulch.

Quinn Southerland.

Lord have mercy.

Tess sat for a moment outside Winder Ranch in the little sedan she had bought after selling Scott's wheelchair van. Her mind was a jumble of impressions, all of them sharp and hard and ugly.

He despised her. His rancor radiated from him like spokes on a bicycle wheel. Though he had conversed with at least some degree of civility throughout their short encounter, every word, every sentence, had been underscored by his contempt. His silvery-blue eyes had never once lost that sheen of scorn when he looked at her.

Tess let out a breath, more disconcerted by the brief meeting than she should be. She had a thick enough skin to withstand a little animosity. Or at least she had always assumed she did, up to this point.

How would she know, though? She had never had much opportunity to find out. Most of the good citizens of Pine Gulch treated her far differently.

Alone in the quiet darkness of her car, she gave a humorless laugh. How many times over the years had she thought how heartily sick she was of being treated like some kind of venerated saint around Pine Gulch? She wanted people to see her as she really was—someone with hopes and dreams and faults. Not only as the tireless caretaker who had dedicated long years of her life to caring for her husband.

She shook her head with another rough laugh. A little middle ground would be nice. Quinn Southerland's outright vilification of her was a little more harsh than she really wanted to face.

He had a right to despise her. She understood his feelings and couldn't blame him for them. She had treated him shamefully in high school. Just the memory, being confronted with the worst part of herself when she hadn't really thought about those things in years, made her squirm as she started her car.

Her treatment of Quinn Southerland had been reprehensible, beyond cruel, and she wanted to cringe away from remembering it. But seeing him again after all these years seemed to set the fragmented, half-forgotten memories shifting and sliding through her mind like jagged plates of glass.

She remembered all of it. The unpleasant rumors she had spread about him; her small, snide comments, delivered at moments when he was quite certain to overhear; the friends and teachers she had turned against him, without even really trying very hard.

She had been a spoiled, petulant bitch, and the memory of it wasn't easy to live with now that she had much more wisdom and maturity and could look back on her terrible behavior through the uncomfortable prism of age and experience.

She fully deserved his contempt, but that knowledge didn't make it much easier to stomach as she drove down the long, winding Winder Ranch driveway and turned onto Cold Creek Road, her headlights gleaming off the leaves that rustled across the road in the October wind.

She loved Jo Winder dearly and had since she was a little girl, when Jo had been patient and kind with the worst piano student any teacher ever had. Tess had promised the woman just the evening before that she would remain one of her hospice caregivers until the end. How on earth was she supposed to keep that vow if it meant being regularly confronted with her own poor actions when she was a silly girl too heedless to care about anyone else's feelings?

The roads were dark and quiet as she drove down Cold Creek Canyon toward her next patient, across town on the west side of Pine Gulch.

Usually she didn't mind the quiet or the solitude, this sense in the still hours of the night that she was the only one around. Even when she was on her way to her most difficult patient, she could find enjoyment in these few moments of peace.

Ed Hardy was a cantankerous eighty-year-old man whose kidneys were failing after years of battling diabetes. He wasn't facing his impending passing with the same dignity or grace as Jo Winder but continued to fight it every step of the way. He was mean-spirited and belligerent, lashing out at anyone who dared remind him he wasn't a twenty-five-year-old wrangler anymore who could rope and ride with the best of them.

Despite his bitterness, she loved the old coot. She loved *all* her home-care patients, even the most difficult. She would miss them, even Ed, when she moved away from Pine Gulch in a month.

She sighed as she drove down Main Street with its darkened businesses and the historic Old West lampposts somebody in the chamber of commerce had talked the town into putting up for the tourists a few years ago.

Except for the years she went to nursing school in Boise and those first brief halcyon months after her marriage, she had lived in this small Idaho town in the west shadow of the Tetons her entire life.

She and Scott had never planned to stay here. Their dreams had been much bigger than a rural community like Pine Gulch could hold.

They had married a month after she graduated from nursing school. He had been a first-year med student, excited about helping people, making a difference in the world. They had talked about opening a clinic in some undeveloped country somewhere, about travel and all the rich buffet of possibilities spreading out ahead of them.

But as she said to Quinn Southerland earlier, sometimes life didn't work out the way one planned. Instead of exotic locales and changing the world, she had brought her husband home to Pine Gulch where she had a support network—friends and family and neighbors who rallied around them.

She pulled into the Hardy driveway, noting the leaves that needed to be raked and the small flower garden that should be put to bed for the winter. Mrs. Hardy had her hands full caring for her husband and his many medical needs. She had a grandson in Idaho Falls who helped a bit with the yard but now that school was back in session, he didn't come as often as he had in the summer.

Tess turned off her engine, shuffling through her mental calendar to see if she could find time in the next few days to come over with a rake.

Her job had never been only about pain management and end-of-life decisions. At least not to her. She knew what it was like to be on the other side of the equation and how very much it could warm the heart when someone showed up unexpectedly with a smile and a cloth and window spray to wash the winter grime she hadn't had time to clean off because her life revolved around caretaking someone else.

That experience as the recipient of service had taught her well that her job was to lift the burdens of the families as much as of her patients.

Even hostile, antagonistic family members like Quinn Southerland.

The wind swirled leaves across the Hardys' cracked driveway as she stepped out of her car. Tess shivered, but she knew it wasn't at the prospect of winter just around the corner or that wind bare-knuckling its way under her jacket, but from remembering the icy cold blue of Quinn's eyes.

Though she wasn't at all eager to encounter him again—or to face the bitter truth of the spoiled brat she had been once—she adored Jo Winder. She couldn't let Quinn's forbidding presence distract her from giving Jo the care she deserved.

Chapter Three

Apparently Pine Gulch's time machine was in fine working order.

Quinn walked into The Gulch and was quite certain he had traveled back twenty years to the first time he walked into the café with his new foster parents. He could clearly remember that day, the smell of frying potatoes and meat, the row of round swivel seats at the old-fashioned soda fountain, the craning necks in the place and the hot gazes as people tried to figure out the identity of the surly, scowling dark-haired kid with Jo and Guff.

Not much had changed. From the tin-stamped ceiling to the long, gleaming mirror that ran the length of the soda fountain to the smell of fried food that seemed to send triglycerides shooting through his veins just from walking in the door.

Even the faces were the same. He could swear the same old-timers still sat in the booth in the corner being served by Donna Archeleta, whose husband, Lou, had always manned the kitchen with great skill and joy. He recognized Mick Malone, Jesse Redbear and Sal Martinez.

And, of course, Donna. She stood by the booth with a pot of coffee in her hand but she just about dropped it all over the floor when she looked up at the sound of the jangling bells on the door to spy him walking into her café.

"Quinn Southerland," she exclaimed, her smoker-husky voice delighted. "As I live and breathe."

"Hey, Donna."

One of Jo's closest friends, Donna had always gone out of her way to be kind to him and to Brant and Cisco. They hadn't always made it easy. The three of them had been the town's resident bad boys back in the day. Well, maybe not Brant, he acknowledged, but he was usually guilty by association, if nothing else.

"I didn't know you were back in town." Donna set the pot down in an empty booth to fold her scrawny arms around him. He hugged her back, wondering when she had gotten frail like Jo.

"Just came in yesterday," he said.

"Why the hell didn't anybody tell me?"

He opened his mouth to answer but she cut him off.

"Oh, no. Jo. Is she…" Her voice trailed off but he could see the anxiety suddenly brim in her eyes, as if she dreaded his response.

He shook his head and forced a smile. "She woke up this morning feistier than ever, craving one of Lou's sweet rolls. Nothing else will do, she told me in no uncertain terms, so she sent me down here first thing so I could pick one up and take it back for her. Since according to East, she hasn't been hungry for much of anything else, I figured I had better hurry right in and grab her one."

Donna's lined and worn features brightened like a gorgeous June morning breaking over the mountains. "You're in luck, hon. I think he's just pullin' a new batch out of the oven. You wait right here and have yourself some coffee while I go back and wrap a half-dozen up for her."

Before he could say a word, she turned a cup over from the setting in the booth and poured him a cup. He laughed at this further evidence that not much had changed, around The Gulch at least.

"I think one, maybe two sweet rolls, are probably enough. Like I said, she hasn't had much of an appetite."

"Well, this way she can warm another up later or save one for the morning, and there will be extras for you and Easton. Now don't you argue with me. I'm doing this, so just sit down and drink your coffee, there's a good boy."

He had to smile in the face of such determination, such eagerness to do something nice for someone she cared about. There were few things he missed about living in Pine Gulch, but that sense of community, belonging to something bigger than yourself, was definitely one of them.

He took a seat at the long bar, joining a few other solo customers who eyed him with curiosity.

Again, he had the strange sense of stepping back into his past. He could still see the small chip in the bottom corner of the mirror where he and Cisco had been roughhousing and accidentally sent a salt shaker flying.

That long-ago afternoon was as clear as his flight in

from Japan the day before—the sick feeling in the pit of his gut as he had faced the wrath of Lou and Donna and the even worse fear when he had to fess up to Guff and Jo. He had only been with them a year, twelve tumultuous months, and had been quite sure they would toss him back into the foster-care system after one mess-up too many.

But Guff hadn't yelled or ordered him to pack his things. Instead, he just sat him down and told one of his rambling stories about a time he had been a young ranch hand with a little too much juice in him and had taken his .22 and shot out the back windows of what he thought was an old abandoned pickup truck, only to find out later it belonged to his boss's brother.

"A man steps up and takes responsibility for his actions," Guff had told him solemnly. That was all he said, but the trust in his brown eyes had completely overwhelmed Quinn. So of course he had returned to The Gulch and offered to work off the cost of replacing the mirror for the Archeletas.

He smiled a little, remembering Lou and Donna's response. "Think we'll just keep that little nick there as a reminder," Lou had said. "But there are always dishes around here to be washed."

He and Cisco had spent about three months of Saturdays and a couple afternoons a week after school in the kitchen with their hands full of soapy water. More than he cared to admit, he had enjoyed those days listening to the banter of the café, all the juicy small-town gossip.

He only had about three or four minutes to replay the memory in his head before Lou Archeleta walked out of the kitchen, his bald head just as shiny as always and his thick salt-and-pepper mustache a bold contrast. The delight on his rough features matched Donna's, warming Quinn somewhere deep inside.

Lou wiped his hand on his white apron before holding it out for a solemn handshake. "Been too long," he said, in that same gruff, no-nonsense way. "Hear Seattle's been pretty good to you."

Quinn shook his hand firmly, aware as he did that much of his success in business derived from watching the integrity and goodness of people like Lou and Donna and the respect with which they had always treated their customers.

"I've done all right," he answered.

"Better than all right. Jo says you've got a big fancy house on the shore and your own private jet."

Technically it was the company's corporate jet. But since he owned the company, he supposed he couldn't debate semantics. "How about you? How's Rick?"

Their son had gone to school with him and graduated a year after him. Tess Jamison's year, actually.

"Good. Good. He's up in Boise these days. He's a plumbing contractor, has himself a real good business. He and his wife gave us our first granddaughter earlier this year." The pride on Lou's work-hardened features was obvious.

"Congratulations."

"Yep, after four boys, they finally got a girl."

Quinn choked on the sip of coffee he'd just taken. "Rick has five kids?"

His mind fairly boggled at the very idea of even one. He couldn't contemplate having enough for a basketball team.

Lou chuckled. "Yep. Started young and threw in a set of twins in there. He's a fine dad, too."

The door chimed, heralding another customer, but Quinn was still reeling at the idea of his old friend raising a gaggle of kids and cleaning out toilets.

Still, an odd little prickle slid down his spine, especially when he heard the old-timers in their regular booth hoot with delight and usher the newcomer over.

"About time you got here," one of the old-timers in the corner called out. "Mick here was sure you was goin' to bail on us today."

"Are you kidding?" an alto female voice answered. "This is my favorite part of working graveyard, the chance to come in here for breakfast and have you all give me a hard time every morning. I don't know what I'll do without it."

Quinn stiffened on the stool. He didn't need to turn to know just who was now sliding into the booth near the regulars. He had last heard that voice at 3:00 a.m. in the dark quiet of the Winder Ranch kitchen.

"Hey, Miss Tess." Lou turned his attention away from bragging about his grandkids to greet the newcomer, confirming what Quinn had already known deep in his bones. "You want your usual?"

"You got it, Lou. I've been dreaming of your veggie omelet all night long. I'm absolutely starving."

"Girl, you need to get yourself something more interesting to fill your nights if all you can dream about is Lou's veggie omelet," called out one of the women from a nearby booth and everybody within earshot laughed.

Everybody but Quinn. She was a regular here, just

like the others, he realized. She was part of the community, and he, once more, was the outsider.

She had always been excellent at reminding him of that.

He couldn't put it off any longer, he knew. With some trepidation, he turned around from the counter to the dining room to face her gaze.

Despite the mirror right in front of him, she must not have been paying attention to the other patrons in the restaurant. He could tell she hadn't known he was there until he turned. He saw the little flash of surprise in her eyes, the slight rise and fall of her slim chest as her breathing hitched.

She covered it quickly with a tight smile and the briefest of waves.

She wasn't pleased to see him. He didn't miss the sudden tension in her posture or the dismay that quickly followed that initial surprise.

Join the club, he thought. Bumping into his worst nightmare two times in less than six hours was twice too many, as far as he was concerned.

He thought he saw something strangely vulnerable flash in those brilliant green eyes for just an instant, then she turned back to the old-timers at the booth with some bright, laughing comment that sounded forced to him.

As he listened to their interaction, it was quickly apparent to him that Tess was a favorite of all of them. No surprise there. She excelled at twisting everybody around her little finger. She had probably been doing the very same thing since she was the age of Lou Archeleta's new granddaughter.

The more the teasing conversation continued, the more

sour his mood turned. She sounded vivacious and funny and charming. Why couldn't anybody but him manage to see past the act to the vicious streak lurking beneath?

When he had just about had all he could stomach, Donna returned with two white bakery bags and a disposable coffee cup with steam curling out the top.

"Here you go, hon. Didn't mean to keep you waiting until Christmas but I got tied up in the back with a phone call from a distributor. There's plenty of extra sweet rolls for you and here's a little joe for the road."

He put away his irritation at Tess and took the offerings from Donna with an affectionate smile, his heart warmer than the cup in his hand at her concern. "Thanks."

"You give that girl a big old kiss from everybody down here at The Gulch. Tell her to hang in there and we're all prayin' for her."

"I'll do that."

"And come back, why don't you, while you're in town. We'll fix you up your favorite chicken-fried steak and have a coze."

"It's a date." He kissed her cheek and headed for the door. Just as he reached it, he heard Tess call his name.

"Wait a minute, will you?" she said.

He schooled his features into a mask of indifference as he turned, loathe for any of the other customers to see how it rankled to see her here still acting like the Pine Gulch Homecoming Queen deigning to have breakfast with her all of her hordes of loyal, adoring subjects.

He didn't want to talk to her. He didn't want to be forced to see how lovely and perky she looked, even in surgical scrubs and even after he knew she had been working all night at a difficult job.

She smelled of vanilla and sunshine and he didn't want to notice that she looked as bright as the morning, how her auburn curls trailed against her slender jawline or the light sprinkle of freckles across her nose or the way her green eyes had that little rim of gold around the edge you only saw if you were looking closely.

He didn't want to see Tess at all, he didn't want to feel like an outsider again in Pine Gulch, and he especially didn't want to have to stand by and do nothing while a woman he loved slipped away, little by little.

"How's Jo this morning?" she asked. "She seemed restless at six when I came to check on her."

As far as he remembered, Tess had never been involved in the high-school drama club. So either she had become a really fabulous actress in the intervening years or her concern for Jo was genuine.

He let out a breath, tamping down his antagonism in light of their shared worry for Jo. "I don't know. To me, she seems better this morning than she was last night when I arrived. But I don't really have a baseline to say what's normal and what's not."

He held up the bakery bag. "She at least had enough energy to ask for Lou's sweet rolls this morning."

"That's excellent. Eating has been hard for her the past few weeks. Seeing you must be giving her a fresh burst of strength."

Was she implying he should have come sooner? He frowned, disliking the guilt swirling around in his gut along with the coffee.

Yeah, he should have come home sooner. If Easton and Jo had been forthright about what was going on, he would have been here weeks ago. They had hid the truth from him but he should have been more intuitive and figured it out.

That didn't mean he appreciated Tess pointing out his negligence. He scowled but she either didn't notice or didn't particularly care.

"It's important that you make sure she doesn't overdo things," Tess said. "I know that's hard to do during those times when she's feeling better. On her good days, she has a tendency to do much more than she really has the strength to tackle. You just have to be careful to ensure she doesn't go overboard."

Her bossy tone brought his dislike simmering to the surface. "Don't try to manage me like you do everybody else in town," he snapped. "I'm not one of your devoted worshippers. We both know I never have been."

For just an instant, hurt flared in her eyes but she quickly blinked it away and tilted that damn perky chin up, her eyes a sudden murky, wintry green.

"This has nothing to do with me," she replied coolly. "It's about Jo. Part of my job as her hospice nurse is to advise her family regarding her care. I can certainly reserve those conversations with Easton if that's what you prefer."

He bristled for just a moment, but the bitter truth of it was, he knew she was right. He needed to put aside how much he disliked this woman for things long in the distant past to focus on his foster mother, who needed him right now.

Tess appeared to genuinely care about Jo. And while he wasn't quite buying such a radical transformation, people could change. He saw it all the time.

Hell, he was a completely different person than he'd been in high school. He wasn't the angry, belligerent hothead with a chip the size of the Tetons on his shoulder anymore, though he was certainly acting like it right now.

It wasn't wholly inconceivable that this caring nurse act was the real thing.

"You're right." He forced the words out, though they scraped his throat raw. "I appreciate the advice. I'm… still struggling with seeing her this way. In my mind, she should still be out on the ranch hurtling fences and rounding up strays."

Her defensive expression softened and she lifted a hand just a little. For one insane moment, he thought she meant to touch his arm in a sympathetic gesture, but she dropped her arm back to her side.

"Wouldn't we all love that?" she said softly. "I'm afraid those days are gone. Right now, we just have to savor every moment with her, even if it's quietly sitting beside her while she sleeps."

She stepped away from him and he was rather horrified at the regret suddenly churning through him. All these conflicting feelings were making him a little crazy.

"I'm off until tonight," she said, "but you'll find Cindy, the day nurse, is wonderful. Even so, tell Easton to call me if she needs anything."

He nodded and pushed past the door into the sunshine.

That imaginary time machine had a few little glitches in it, he thought as he pulled out of the parking lot and headed back toward Cold Creek Canyon.

He had just exchanged several almost civil words with Tess Jamison Claybourne, something that a dozen years ago would have seemed just as impossible as imagining that someday he would be able to move past the ugliness in his past to run his own very successful company.

Chapter Four

"Do you remember that time you boys stayed out with the Walker sisters an hour past curfew?"

"I'm going to plead the fifth on that one," Quinn said lazily, though he did indeed remember Sheila Walker and some of her more acrobatic skills.

"I remember it," Jo said. "The door was locked and you couldn't get back in so you rascals tried to sneak in a window, remember that? Guff heard a noise downstairs and since he was half-asleep and didn't realize you boys hadn't come home yet, he thought it might be burglars."

Jo chuckled. "He took the baseball bat he kept by the side of the bed and went down and nearly beaned the three of you as you were trying to sneak in the window."

He smiled at the memory of Brant's guilt and

Cisco's smart-aleck comments and Guff's stern reprim-
and to all of them.

"I can't believe Guff told you about that. It was
supposed to be a secret between us males."

Her mouth lifted a little at the edges. "Guff didn't
keep secrets from me. Don't you know better than that?
He used to say whatever he couldn't tell me, he would
rather not know himself."

Jo's voice changed when she talked about her late
husband. The tone was softer, more rounded, and her
love sounded in every word.

He squeezed her fingers. What a blessing for both
Guff and Jo that they had found each other, even if it
had been too late in life for the children they had both
always wanted. Though they married in their forties,
they had figured out a way to build the family they
wanted by taking in foster children who had nowhere
else to go.

"I suppose that's as good a philosophy for a marriage
as any," he said.

"Yes. That and the advice of Lyndon B. Johnson.
Only two things are necessary to keep one's wife happy,
Guff used to say. One is to let her think she is having
her own way. The other, to let her have it."

He laughed, just as he knew she intended. Jo smiled
along with him and lifted her face to the late-morning
sunshine. He checked to make sure the colorful throw
was still tucked across her lap, though it was a beautiful autumn day, warmer than usual for October.

They sat on Adirondack chairs canted just so in the back
garden of Winder Ranch for a spectacular view of the west
slope of the Tetons. Surrounding them were mums and

yarrow and a few other hardy plants still hanging on. Most of the trees were nearly bare but a few still clung tightly to their leaves. As he remembered, the stubborn elms liked to hang on to theirs until the most messy, inconvenient time, like just before the first hard snowfall, when it became a nightmare trying to rake them up.

Mindful of Tess's advice, he was keeping a careful eye on Jo and her stamina level. So far, she seemed to be managing her pain. She seemed content to sit in her garden and bask in the unusual warmth.

He wasn't used to merely sitting. In Seattle, he always had someone clamoring for his attention. His assistant, his board of directors, his top-level executives. Someone always wanted a slice of his time.

Quinn couldn't quite ascertain whether he found a few hours of enforced inactivity soothing or frustrating. But he did know he savored this chance to store away a few more precious memories of Jo.

She lifted her thin face to the sunshine. "We won't have too many more days like this, will we? Before we know it, winter will be knocking on the door."

That latent awareness that she probably wouldn't make it even to Thanksgiving—her favorite holiday—pierced him.

He tried to hide his reaction but Jo had eyes like a red-tailed hawk and was twice as focused.

"Stop that," she ordered, her mouth suddenly stern.

"What?"

"Feeling sorry for me, son."

He folded her hand in his, struck again by the frailty of it, the pale skin and the thin bones and the tiny blue veins pulsing beneath the papery surface.

"You want the truth, I'm feeling more sorry for myself than you."

Her laugh startled a couple of sparrows from the bird feeder hanging in the aspens. "You always did have a bit of a selfish streak, didn't you?"

"Damn right." He managed a tiny grin in response to her teasing. "And I'm selfish enough to wish you could stick around forever."

"For your sake and the others, I'm sorry for that. But don't be sad on my account, my dear. I have missed my husband sorely every single, solitary moment of the past three years. Soon I'll be with him again and won't have to miss him anymore. Why would anyone possibly pity me?"

He would have given a great deal for even a tiny measure of her faith. He hadn't believed much in a just and loving God since the nightmare day his parents died.

"I only have one regret," Jo went on.

He made a face. "Only one?" He could have come up with a couple dozen of his own regrets, sitting here in the sunshine on a quiet Cold Creek morning.

"Yes. I'm sorry my children—and that's what you all are, you know—have never found the kind of joy and love Guff and I had."

"I don't think many people have," he answered. "What is it they say? Often imitated, never duplicated? What the two of you had was something special. Unique."

"Special, yes. Unique, not at all. A good marriage just takes lots of effort on both parts." She tilted her head and studied him carefully. "You've never even been serious about a woman, have you? I know you date plenty of beautiful women up there in Seattle. What's wrong with them all?"

He gave a rough laugh. "Not a thing, other than I have no desire to get married."

"Ever?"

"Marriage isn't for me, Jo. Not with my family history."

"Oh, poof."

He laughed at the unexpectedness of the word. "Poof?"

"You heard me. You're just making excuses. Never thought I raised any of my boys to be cowards."

"I'm not a coward," he exclaimed.

"What else would you call it?"

He didn't answer, though a couple of words that came immediately to mind were more along the lines of *smart* and *self-protective.*

"Yes, you had things rough," Jo said after a moment. "I'm not saying you didn't. It breaks my heart what some people do to their families in the name of love. But plenty of other people have things rough and it doesn't stop them from living their life. Why, take Tess, for instance."

He gave a mental groan. Bad enough that he couldn't seem to stop thinking about her all morning. He didn't need Jo bringing her up now. Just the sound of her name stirred up those weird, conflicting emotions inside him all over again. Anger and that subtle, insistent, frustrating attraction.

He pushed them all away. "What do you mean, *take Tess?*"

"That girl. Now *she* has an excuse to lock her heart away and mope around feeling sorry for herself for the rest of her life. But does she? No. You'll never find a happier soul in all your days. Why, what she's been through would have crushed most women. Not our Tess."

What could she possibly have been through that Jo deemed so traumatic? She was a pampered princess, daughter of one of the wealthiest men in town, the town's bank president, apparently adored by everyone.

She couldn't know what it was like to have to call the police on your own father or hold your mother as she breathed her last.

Before he could ask Jo to explain, she began to cough—raspy, wet hacking that made his own chest hurt just listening to it.

She covered her mouth with a folded handkerchief from her pocket as the coughing fit went on for what seemed an eon. When she pulled the cloth away, he didn't miss the red spots speckling the white linen.

"I'm going to carry you inside and call Easton."

Jo shook her head. "No," she choked out. "Will pass. Just…minute."

He gave her thirty more seconds, then reached for his cell phone. He started to hit Redial to reach Easton when he realized Jo's coughs were dwindling.

"Told you…would pass," she said after a moment. During the coughing attack, what little color there was in her features had seeped out and she looked as if she might blow away if the wind picked up even a knot or two.

"Let's get you inside."

She shook her head. "I like the sunshine."

He sat helplessly beside her while she coughed a few more times, then folded the handkerchief and stuck it back into her pocket.

"Sorry about that," she murmured after a painful moment. "I so wish you didn't have to see me like this."

He wrapped an arm around her frail shoulders and

pulled her close to him, planting a kiss on her springy gray curls.

"We don't have to talk. Just rest. We can stay for a few more moments and enjoy the sunshine."

She smiled and settled against him and they sat in contented silence.

For those few moments, he was deeply grateful he had come. As difficult as it had been to rearrange his schedule and delegate as many responsibilities as he could to the other executives at Southerland, he wouldn't have missed this moment for anything.

With his own mother, he hadn't been given the luxury of saying goodbye. She had been unconscious by the time he could reach her.

He supposed that played some small part in his insistence that he stay here to the end with Jo, as difficult as it was to face, as if he could atone in some small way for all he hadn't been able to do for his own mother as a frightened kid.

Her love of sunshine notwithstanding, Jo lasted outside only another fifteen minutes before she had a coughing fit so intense it left her pale and shaken. He didn't give her a choice this time, simply scooped her into his arms and carried her inside to her bedroom.

"Rest there and I'll find Easton to help you."

"Bother. She…has enough…to do. Just need water and…minute to catch my breath."

He went for a glass of water and returned to Jo's bedroom with it, then sent a quick text to Easton explaining the situation.

"I can see you sending out an SOS over there," Jo muttered with a dark look at the phone in his hand.

"Who, me? I was just getting in a quick game of solitaire while I wait for you to stop coughing."

She snorted at the lie and shook her head. "You didn't need to call her. I hate being so much of a nuisance to everyone."

He finished the text and covered her hand with his. "Serves us right for all the bother we gave you."

"I think you boys used to stay up nights just thinking about new ways to get into trouble, didn't you?"

"We had regular meetings every afternoon, just to brainstorm."

"I don't doubt it." She smiled weakly. "At least by the middle of high school you settled down some. Though there was that time senior year you got kicked off the baseball team. That nonsense about cheating, which I know you would never do, and so I tried to tell the coach but he wouldn't listen. You never did tell us what that was really all about."

He frowned. He could have told her what it had been about. Tess Jamison and more of her lies about him. If anyone had stayed up nights trying to come up with ways to make someone else's life harder, it would have been Tess. She had made as much trouble as she could for him, for reasons he still didn't understand.

"High school was a long time ago. Why don't I tell you about my latest trip to Cambodia when I visited Angkor Wat?"

He described the ancient temple complex that had been unknown to the outside world until 1860, when a French botanist stumbled upon it. He was describing the nearby city of Angkor Thom when he looked down and saw her eyes were closed, her breathing regular.

He arranged a knit throw over her and slipped off her shoes, which didn't elicit even a hint of a stir out of her. That she could fall asleep so instantaneously worried him and he hoped their short excursion outside hadn't been too much for her.

He closed the door behind him just as he heard the bang of the screen door off the kitchen, then the thud of Easton's boots on the tile.

Chester rose from his spot in a sunbeam and greeted her with delight, his tired old body wiggling with glee.

She stripped off her work gloves and patted him. "Sorry it took me a while. We were up repairing a fence in the west pasture."

"I'm sorry I called you in for nothing. She seems to be resting now. But she was coughing like crazy earlier, leaving blood specks behind."

Easton blew out a breath and swiped a strand of hair that had fallen out of her long ponytail. "She's been doing that lately. Tess says it's to be expected."

"I'm sorry I bugged you for no reason."

"I was ready to break for lunch. I would have been here in about fifteen minutes anyway. I can't tell you what a relief it is to have you here so I know someone is with her. I'm always within five minutes of the house but I can't be here all the time. I hate when I have to leave her, but sometimes I can't help it. The ranch doesn't run itself."

Though Winder Ranch wasn't as huge an operation as the Daltons up the canyon a ways, it was still a big undertaking for one woman still in her twenties, even if she did have a couple ranch hands and a ranch foreman who had been with the Winders since Easton's father died in a car accident that also killed his wife.

"Why don't I fix you some lunch while you're here?" he offered. "It's my turn after last night, isn't it?"

She sent him a sidelong look. "The CEO of Southerland Shipping making me a bologna sandwich? How can I resist an offer like that?"

"Turkey is my specialty but I suppose I can swing bologna."

"Either one would be great. I'll go check on Jo and be right back."

She returned before he had even found all the ingredients.

"Still asleep?" he asked.

"Yes. She was smiling in her sleep and looked so at peace, I didn't have the heart to wake her."

"Sit down. I'll be done here in a moment."

She sat at the kitchen table with a tall glass of Pepsi and they chatted about the ranch and the upcoming roundup in the high country and the cost of beef futures while he fixed sandwiches for both of them.

He presented hers with a flourish and she accepted it gratefully.

"What time does the day nurse come again?" he asked.

"Depends on the nurse, but usually about 1:00 p.m. and then again at five or six o'clock."

"And there are three nurses who rotate?"

"Yes. They're all wonderful but Tess is Jo's favorite."

He paused to swallow a bite of his sandwich then tried to make his voice sound casual and uninterested. "What's her story?" he asked.

"Who? Tess?"

"Jo said something about her that made me curious. She said Tess had it rough."

"You could say that."

He waited for Easton to elucidate but she remained frustratingly silent and he had to take a sip of soda to keep from grinding his back teeth together. The Winder women—and he definitely counted Easton among that number since her mother had been Guff's sister—could drive him crazy with their reticence that they seemed to invoke only at the most inconvenient times.

"What's been so rough?" he pressed. "When I knew Tess, she had everything a woman could want. Brains, beauty, money."

"None of that helped her very much with everything that came after, did it?" Easton asked quietly.

"I have no idea. You haven't told me what that was."

He waited while Easton took another bite of her sandwich before continuing. "I guess you figured out she married Scott, right?"

He shrugged. "That was a foregone conclusion, wasn't it? They dated all through high school."

He had actually always liked Scott Claybourne. Tall and blond and athletic, Scott had been amiable to Quinn if not particularly friendly—until their senior year, when Scott had inexplicably beat the crap out of Quinn one warm April night, with veiled references to some supposed misconduct of Quinn's toward Tess.

More of her lies, he had assumed, and had pitied the bastard for being so completely taken in by her.

"They were only married three or four months, still newlyweds, really," Easton went on, "when he was in a bad car accident."

He frowned. "Car accident? I thought Tess told me he died of pneumonia."

"Technically, he did, just a couple of years ago. But he lived for several years after the accident, though he was permanently disabled from it. He had a brain injury and was in a pretty bad way."

He stared at Easton, trying to make the jaggedly formed pieces of the puzzle fit together. Tess had stuck around Pine Gulch for *years* to deal with her husband's brain injury? He couldn't believe it, not of her.

"She cared for him tirelessly, all that time," Easton said quietly. "From what I understand, he required total care. She had to feed him, dress him, bathe him. He was almost more like her kid than her husband, you know."

"He never recovered from the brain injury?"

"A little but not completely. He was in a wheelchair and lost the ability to talk from the injury. It was so sad. I just remember how nice he used to be to us younger kids. I don't know how much was going on inside his head but Tess talked to him just like normal and she seemed to understand what sounded like grunts and moans to me."

The girl he had known in high school had been only interested in wearing her makeup just so and buying the latest fashion accessories. And making his life miserable, of course.

He couldn't quite make sense of what Easton was telling him.

"I saw them once at the grocery store when he had a seizure, right there in frozen foods," Easton went on. "It scared the daylights out of me, let me tell you, but Tess just acted like it was a normal thing. She was so calm and collected through the whole thing."

"That's rough."

She nodded. "A lot of women might have shoved away from the table when they saw the lousy hand they'd been dealt, would have just walked away right then. Tess was young, just out of nursing school. She had enough medical experience that I have to think she could guess perfectly well what was ahead for them, but she stuck it out all those years."

He didn't like the compassion trickling through him for her. Somehow things seemed more safe, more ordered, before he had learned that perhaps she hadn't spent the past dozen years figuring out more ways to make him loathe her.

"People in town grew to respect and admire her for the loving care she gave Scott, even up to the end. When she moves to Portland in a few weeks, she's going to leave a real void in Pine Gulch. I'm not the only one who will miss her."

"She's leaving?"

He again tried to be casual with the question, but Easton had known him since he was fourteen. She sent him a quick, sidelong look.

"She's selling her house and taking a job at a hospital there. I can't blame her. Around here, she'll always be the sweet girl who took care of her sick husband for so long. Saint Tess. That's what people call her."

He nearly fell off his chair at that one. Tess Jamison Claybourne was a saint like he played center field for the Mariners.

Easton pushed back from the table. "I'd better check on Jo one more time, then get back to work." She paused. "You know, if you have more questions about Tess, you could ask her. She should be back tonight."

He didn't want to know more about Tess. He didn't want anything to do with her. He wanted to go back to the safety of ignorance. Despising her was much easier when he could keep her frozen in his mind as the manipulative little witch she had been at seventeen.

Chapter Five

"You haven't heard a single word I've said for the past ten minutes, have you?"

Tess jerked her attention back to her mother as they worked side by side in Ed Hardy's yard. Her mother knelt in the mulchy layer of fallen leaves, snipping and digging to ready Dorothy Hardy's flower garden for the winter, while Tess was theoretically supposed to be raking leaves. Her pile hadn't grown much, she had to admit.

"I heard some of it." She managed a rueful smile. "The occasional word here and there."

Maura Jamison raised one delicately shaped eyebrow beneath her floppy gardening hat. "I'm sorry my stories are so dull. I can go back to telling them to the cat, when he'll deign to listen."

She winced. "It's not your story that's to blame.

I'm just…distracted today. But I'll listen now. Sorry about that."

Her mother gave her a careful look. "I think it's my turn to listen. What's on your mind, honey? Scott?"

Tess blinked at the realization that except for those few moments when Quinn had asked her about Scott the night before, she hadn't thought about her husband in several days.

A tiny measure of guilt niggled at her but she pushed it away. She refused to feel guilty for that. Scott would have wanted her to move on with her life and she had no guilt for her dealings with her husband.

Still, she didn't think she could tell her mother she was obsessing about Quinn Southerland.

"Mom, was I a terrible person in high school?" she asked instead.

Maura's eyes widened with surprise and Tess sent a tiny prayer to heaven, not for the first time, that she could age as gracefully as her mother. At sixty-five, Maura was active and vibrant and still as lovely as ever, even in gardening clothes and her floppy hat. The auburn curls Tess had inherited were shot through with gray but it didn't make Maura look old, only exotic and interesting, somehow.

Maura pursed her lips. "As I remember, you were a very good person. Not perfect, certainly, but who is, at that age?"

"I thought I was. Perfect, I mean. I thought I was doing everything right. Why wouldn't I? I had 4.0 grades, I was the head cheerleader, the student body president. I volunteered at the hospital in Idaho Falls and went to church on Sundays and was generally kind to children and small pets."

"What's happened to make you think about those days?"

She sighed, remembering the antipathy in a certain pair of silvery blue eyes. "Quinn Southerland is back in town."

Her mother's brow furrowed for a moment, then smoothed again. "Oh, right. He was one of Jo and Guff's foster boys, wasn't he? Which one is he?"

"Not the army officer or the adventurer. He's the businessman. The one who runs a shipping company out of Seattle."

"Oh, yes. I remember him. He was the dark, brooding, cute one, right?"

"Mother!"

Maura gave her an innocent sort of look. "What did I say? He *was* cute, wasn't he? I always thought he looked a little like James Dean around the eyes. Something in that smoldering look of his."

Oh, yes, Tess remembered it well.

After leaning the rake against a tree, she knelt beside her mother and began pulling up the dead stalks of cosmos. Every time she worked with her hands in the dirt, she couldn't help thinking how very much her existence the past eight years was like a flower garden in winter, waiting, waiting, for life to spring forth.

"I was horrible to him, Mom. Really awful."

"You? I can't believe that."

"Believe it. He just… He brought out the absolute worst in me."

Her mother sat back on her heels, the gardening forgotten. "Whatever did you do to the poor boy?"

She didn't want to correct her mother, but to her

mind Quinn had never seemed like a boy. At least not like the other boys in Pine Gulch.

"I don't even like to think about it all," she admitted. "Basically I did whatever I could to set him down a peg or two. I did my best to turn people against him. I would make snide comments to him and about him and started unsubstantiated rumors about him. I played devil's advocate, just for the sake of argument, whenever he would express any kind of opinion in a class."

Her mother looked baffled. "What on earth did he do to you to make you act in such a way?"

"Nothing. That's the worst part. I thought he was arrogant and disrespectful and I didn't like him but I was…fascinated by him."

Which quite accurately summed up her interaction with him in the early hours of the morning, but she decided not to tell her mother that.

"He was a handsome boy," Maura said. "I imagine many of the girls at school had the same fascination."

"They did." She grabbed the garden shears and started cutting back Dorothy's day lily foliage. "You know how it is whenever someone new moves into town. He seems infinitely better-looking, more interesting, more *everything* than the boys around town that you've grown up with since kindergarten."

She had been just as intrigued as the other girls, fascinated by this surly, angry, rough-edged boy. Rumors had swirled around when he first arrived that he had been involved in some kind of murder investigation. She still didn't know if any of them were true—she really couldn't credit Jo and Guff bringing someone with that kind of a past into their home.

But back then, that hint of danger only made him seem more appealing. She just knew Quinn made her feel different than any other boy in town.

Tess had tried to charm him, as she had been effortlessly doing with every male who entered her orbit since she was old enough to bat her eyelashes. He had at first ignored her efforts and then actively rebuffed them.

She hadn't taken with grace and dignity his rejection or his grim amusement at her continued efforts to draw his attention. She flushed, remembering.

"He wasn't interested in any of us, especially not me. I couldn't understand why he had to be so contrary. I hated it. You know how I was. I wanted everything in my life to go exactly how I arranged it."

"You're like your father that way," Maura said with a soft smile for her husband of thirty-five years whom they both missed dearly.

"I guess. I just know I was petty and spiteful to Quinn when he wouldn't fall into line with the way I wanted things to go. I was awful to him. Really awful. Whenever I was around him, I felt like this alien life force had invaded my body, this manipulative, conniving witch. Scarlett O'Hara with pom-poms."

Her mother laughed. "You're much prettier than that Vivien Leigh ever was."

"But every bit as vindictive and self-absorbed as her character in the movie."

For several moments, she busied herself with garden shears. Maura seemed content with the silence and her introspection, which had always been one of the things Tess loved best about her mother.

"I don't even want to tell you all the things I did," she

finally said. "The worst thing is, I got him kicked off the baseball team when he was a senior and I was a junior."

"Tessa Marie. What on earth did you do?"

She burned with shame at the memory. "We had advanced placement history together. Amaryllis Wentworth."

"Oh, I remember her," her mother exclaimed. "Bitter and mean and suspicious old bat. I don't know why the school board didn't fire her twenty-five years before you were even in school. You would think someone who chooses teaching as an avocation would at least enjoy the company of young people."

"Right. And the only thing she hated worse than teenage girls was teenage boys."

"What happened?"

She wished she could block the memory out but it was depressingly clear, from the chalkboard smell in Wentworth's room to the afternoon spring sunlight filtering through the tall school windows.

"We both happened to have missed school on the same day, which happened to be one of her brutal pop quizzes, so we had to take a makeup. We were the only ones in the classroom except for Miss Wentworth."

Careful to avoid her mother's gaze, she picked up an armload of garden refuse and carried it to the wheelbarrow. "I knew the material but I was curious about whether Quinn did so I looked at his test answers. He got everything right except a question about the Teapot Dome scandal. I don't know why I did it. Pure maliciousness on my part. But I changed my answer, which I knew was right, to the same wrong one he had put down."

"Honey!"

"I know, right? It was awful of me. One of the worst things I've ever done. Of course, Miss Wentworth accused him of cheating. It was his word against mine. The juvenile delinquent with the questionable attitude or the student body president, a junior who already had offers of a full-ride scholarship to nursing school. Who do you think everybody wanted to believe?"

"Oh, Tess."

"My only defense is that I never expected things to go that far. I thought maybe Miss Wentworth would just yell at him, but when she went right to the principal, I didn't know how to make it right. I should have stepped forward when he was kicked off the baseball team but I…was too much of a coward."

She couldn't tell her mother the worst of it. Even she couldn't quite believe the depths to which she had sunk in her teenage narcissism, but she remembered it all vividly.

A few days later, prompted by guilt and shame, she had tried to talk to him and managed to corner him in an empty classroom. They had argued and he had called her a few bad names, justifiably so.

She still didn't know what she'd been thinking— why this time would be any different—but she thought she saw a little spark of attraction in his eyes when they were arguing. She had been hopelessly, mortifyingly foolish enough to try to kiss him and he had pushed her away, so hard she knocked over a couple of chairs as she stumbled backward.

Humiliated and outraged, she had then made things much, much worse and twisted the story, telling her boyfriend Scott that Quinn had come on to her, that he had been so angry at being kicked off the baseball team that he had come for revenge and tried to force himself on her.

She screwed her eyes shut. Scott had reacted just as she had expected, with teenage bluster and bravado and his own twisted sense of chivalry. He and several friends from the basketball team had somehow separated Quinn from Brant and Cisco and taken him beneath the football bleachers, then proceeded to beat the tar out of him.

No wonder he despised her. She loathed that selfish, manipulative girl just as much.

"So he's back," Maura said. "Is he staying at the ranch?"

She nodded. "I hate seeing him. He makes me feel sixteen and stupid all over again. If I didn't love Jo so much, I would try to assign her to another hospice nurse."

Maura sat back on her heels, showing her surprise at her daughter's vehemence. "Our Saint Tess making a selfish decision? That doesn't sound like you."

Tess made a face. "You know I hate that nickname."

Her mother touched her arm, leaving a little spot of dirt on her work shirt. "I know you do, dear. And I'll be honest, as a mother who is nothing but proud of the woman you've become and what you have done with your life, it's a bit refreshing to find out you're subject to the occasional human folly just like the rest of us."

Everyone in town saw her as some kind of martyr for staying with Scott all those years, but they didn't know the real her. The woman who had indulged in bouts of self-pity, who had cried out her fear and frustration, who had felt trapped in a marriage that never even had a chance to start.

She had stayed with Scott because she loved him and

because he needed her, not because she was some saintly, perfect, flawless angel.

No one knew her. Not her mother or her friends or the morning crowd at The Gulch.

She didn't like to think that Quinn Southerland might just have the most honest perspective around of the real Tess Jamison Claybourne.

That evening, Tess kept her fingers crossed the entire drive to Winder Ranch, praying she wouldn't encounter him.

She had fretted about him all day, worrying what she might say when she saw him again. She considered it a huge advantage, at least in this case, that she worked the graveyard shift. Most of her visits were in the dead of night, when Quinn by rights should be sleeping. She would have a much better chance of avoiding him than if she stopped by during daylight hours.

The greatest risk she faced of bumping into him was probably now at the start of her shift than, say, 4:00 a.m.

Wouldn't it be lovely if he were away from the ranch or busy helping Easton with something or tied up with some kind of conference call to Seattle?

She could only dream, she supposed. More than likely, he would be right there waiting for her, ready to impale her with that suspicious, bad-tempered glare the moment she stepped out of the car.

She let out a breath as she turned onto the long Winder Ranch access drive and headed up toward the house. She could at least be calm and collected, even if he tried to goad her or made any derogatory comments. He certainly didn't need to discover he possessed such power to upset her.

He wasn't waiting for her on the porch, but it was a near thing. The instant she rang the doorbell of Winder Ranch, the door jerked open and Quinn stood inside looking frazzled, his dark hair disheveled slightly, his navy blue twill shirt untucked, a hint of afternoon shadow on his cheeks.

He looked a little disreputable and entirely yummy.

"It's about time!" he exclaimed, an odd note of relief in his voice. "I've been watching for you for the past half hour."

"You...have?"

She almost looked behind her to see if someone a little more sure of a welcome had wandered in behind her.

"I thought you were supposed to be here at eight."

She checked her watch and saw it was only eight-thirty. "I made another stop first. What's wrong?"

He raked a hand through his hair, messing it further. "I don't know the hell I'm supposed to do. Easton had to run to Idaho Falls to meet with the ranch accountant. She was supposed to be back an hour ago but she just called and said she'd been delayed and won't be back for another couple of hours."

"What's going on? Is Jo having another of her breathing episodes? Or is it the coughing?"

Tess hurried out of her jacket and started to rush toward her patient's room but Quinn grabbed her arm at the elbow.

Despite her worry for Jo, heat scorched her nerve endings at the contact, at the feel of his warm hand against her skin.

"She's not there. She's in the kitchen."

At her alarmed look, he shook his head. "It's none of those things. She's fine, physically, anyway. But she won't listen to reason. I never realized the woman could be so blasted stubborn."

"A trait she obviously does not share with anyone else here," she murmured.

He gave her a dark look. "She's being completely ridiculous. She suddenly has this harebrained idea. Absolute insanity. She wants to go out for a moonlight ride on one of the horses and it's suddenly all she can talk about."

She stared, nonplussed. "A horseback ride?"

"Yeah. Do you think the cancer has affected her rational thinking? I mean, what's gotten into her? It's after eight, for heaven's sake."

"It's a bit difficult to go on a moonlit ride in the middle of the afternoon," she pointed out.

"Don't you take her side!" He sounded frustrated and on edge and more than a little frazzled.

She hid her smile that the urbane, sophisticated executive could change so dramatically over one simple request. "I'm not taking anyone's side. Why does she suddenly want to go tonight?"

"Her window faces east."

That was all he said, as if everything was now crystal clear. "And?" she finally prompted.

"And she happened to see that huge full moon coming up an hour or so ago. She says it's her favorite kind of night. She and Guff used to ride up to Windy Lake during the full moon whenever they could. It can be clear as day up in the mountains on full moons like this."

"Windy Lake?"

"It's above the ranch, about half a mile into the forest service land. Takes about forty minutes to ride there."

"And Tess is determined to go?"

"She says she can't miss the chance, since it's her last harvest moon."

The sudden bleakness in the silver-blue of his eyes tugged at her sympathy and she was astonished by the impulse to touch his arm and offer whatever small comfort she could.

She curled her fingers into a fist, knowing he wouldn't welcome the gesture. Not from her.

"She's not strong enough for that," he went on. "I *know* she's not. We were sitting out in the garden today and she lasted less than an hour before she had to lie down, and then she slept for the rest of the day. I can't see any way in hell she has the strength to sit on a horse, even for ten minutes."

Her job as a hospice nurse often required using a little creative problem-solving. Clients who were dying could have some very tricky wishes toward the end. But her philosophy was that if what they wanted was at all within reach, it was up to her and their family members to make it happen.

"What if you rode together on horseback?" she suggested. "You could help her. Support her weight, make sure she's not overdoing."

He stared at her as if she'd suddenly stepped into her old cheerleader skirt and started yelling, "We've got spirit, yes we do."

"Tell me you're not honestly thinking she could handle this!" he exclaimed. "It's completely insane."

"Not completely, Quinn. Not if she wants to do it. Jo is right. This is her last harvest moon and if she wants to enjoy it from Windy Lake, I think she ought to have that opportunity. It seems a small enough thing to give her."

He opened his mouth to object, then closed it again. In his eyes, she saw worry and sorrow for the woman who had taken him in, given him a home, loved him.

"It might be good for her," Tess said gently.

"And it might finish her off." He said the words tightly, as if he didn't want to let them out.

"That's her choice, though, isn't it?"

He took several deep breaths and she could see his struggle, something she faced often providing end-of-life care. On the one hand, he loved his foster mother and wanted to do everything he could to make her happy and comfortable and fulfill all her last wishes.

On the other, he wanted to protect her and keep her around as long as he could.

The effort to hold back her fierce urge to touch him, console him, almost overwhelmed her. She supposed she shouldn't find it so surprising. She was a nurturer, which was why she went into nursing in the first place, long before she ever knew that Scott's accident would test her caregiving skills and instincts to the limit.

"You don't have to take her, though, especially if you don't feel it's the right thing for her. I'll see if I can talk her out of it," she offered. She took a step toward the kitchen, but his voice stopped her.

"Wait."

She turned back to find him pinching the skin at the bridge of his nose.

"You're right," he said after a long moment, dropping his hand. "It's her choice. She's a grown woman, not a child. I can't treat her like one, even if I do want to protect her from…the inevitable. If she wants this, I'll find a way to make it happen."

The determination in his voice arrowed right to her heart and she smiled. "You're a good son, Quinn. You're just what Jo needs right now."

"You're coming with us, to make sure she's not over-doing things."

"Me?"

"The only way I can agree to this insanity is if we have a medical expert close at hand, just in case."

"I don't think that's a good idea."

"Why not? Can't your other patients spare you?"

That would have been a convenient excuse, but unfortunately in this case, she faced a slow night, with only Tess and two other patients, one who only required one quick check in the night, several hours away.

"That's not the issue," she admitted.

"What is it, then? Don't you think she would be better off to have a nurse along?"

"Maybe. Probably. But not necessarily this particular nurse."

"Why not?"

"I'm not really much of a rider," she confessed, with the same sense of shame as if she were admitting stealing heart medicine from little old ladies. Around Pine Gulch, she supposed the two crimes were roughly parallel in magnitude.

"Really?"

"My family lived in town and we never had horses," she said, despising the defensive note in her voice. "I haven't had a lot of experience."

She didn't add that she had an irrational fear of them

after being bucked off at a cousin's house when she was seven, then later that summer she had seen a cowboy badly injured in a fall at an Independence Day rodeo. Since then, she had done her best to avoid equines whenever possible.

"This is a pretty easy trail that takes less than an hour. You should be okay, don't you think?"

How could she possibly tell him she was terrified, especially after she had worked to persuade him it would be all right for Jo? She couldn't, she decided. Better to take one for the team, for Jo's sake.

"Fine. You saddle the horses and I'll get Jo ready."

Heaven help them all.

Chapter Six

"Let me know if you need me to slow down," Quinn said half an hour later to the frail woman who sat in front of him astride one of the biggest horses in the pasture, a rawboned roan gelding named Russ.

She felt angular and thin in his arms, all pointed elbows and bony shoulders. But Tess had been right, she was ecstatic about being on horseback again, about being outside in the cold October night under the pines. Jo practically quivered with excitement, more alive and joyful than he had seen her since his return to Cold Creek.

It smelled of fall in the mountains, of sun-warmed dirt, of smoke from a distant neighbor's fire, of layers of fallen leaves from the scrub oak and aspens that dotted the mountainside.

The moon hung heavy and full overhead, huge and glowing in the night and Suzy and Jack, Easton's younger cow dogs, raced ahead of them. Chester probably would have enjoyed the adventure but Quinn had worried that, just like Jo, his old bones weren't quite up to the journey.

"This is perfect. Oh, Quinn, thank you, my dear. You have no idea the gift you've given me."

"You're welcome," he said gruffly, warmed despite his lingering worry.

In truth, he didn't know who was receiving the greater gift. This seemed a rare and precious time with Jo and he was certain he would remember forever the scents and the sounds of the night—of tack jingling on the horses and a great northern owl hooting somewhere in the forest and the night creatures that peeped and chattered around them.

He glanced over his shoulder to where Tess rode behind them.

Among the three of them, she seemed to be the one *least* enjoying the ride. She bounced along on one of the ranch's most placid mares. Every once in a while, he looked back and the moonlight would illuminate a look of grave discomfort on her features. If he could see her hands in the darkness, he was quite certain they would be white-knuckled on the reins.

He should be enjoying her misery, given his general dislike for the woman. Mostly he just felt guilty for dragging her along, though he had to admit to a small measure of glee to discover something she hadn't completely mastered.

In school, Tess had been the consummate perfectionist. She always had to be the first one finished with tests and assignments, she hated showing up anywhere with a hair out of place and she delighted in being the kind of annoying classmate who tended to screw up the curve for everybody else.

Knowing she wasn't an expert at everything made her seem a little more human, a little more approachable.

He glanced back again and saw her shifting in the saddle, her body tight and uncomfortable.

"How are you doing back there?" he asked.

In the pale glow of the full moon, he could just make out the slit of her eyes as she glared. "Fine. Swell. If I break my neck and die, I'm blaming you."

He laughed out loud, which earned him a frown from Jo.

"You didn't need to drag poor Tess up here with us," she reprimanded in the same tone of voice she had used when he was fifteen and she caught him teasing Easton for something or other. He could still vividly remember the figurative welts on his hide as she had verbally taken a strip off him.

"She's a big girl," Quinn said in a voice too low for Tess to overhear. "She didn't have to come."

"You're a hard man to say no to."

"If anyone could do it, Tess would find a way. Anyway, we'll be there in a few more moments."

Jo looked over his shoulder at Tess, then shook her head. "Poor thing. She obviously hasn't had as much experience riding as you and Easton and the boys. She's a good sport to come anyway."

He risked another look behind him and thought he heard her mumbling something under her breath involving creative ways she intended to make him pay for this.

Despite the lingering sadness in knowing he was fulfilling a last wish for someone he loved so dearly, Quinn couldn't help his smile.

He definitely wouldn't forget this night anytime soon.

"She's doing all right," he said to Jo.

"You're a rascal, Quinn Southerland," she chided. "You always have been."

He couldn't disagree. He couldn't have been an easy kid to love when he had been so belligerent and angry, lashing out at everyone in his pain. He hugged Jo a little more tightly for just a moment until they reached the trailhead for Windy Lake, really just a clearing where they could leave the horses before taking the narrow twenty-yard trail to the lakeshore.

"This might get a little bit tricky," he said. "Let me dismount first and then I'll help you down."

"I can still get down from a horse by myself," she protested. "I'm not a complete invalid."

He just shook his head in exasperation and slid off the horse. He grabbed the extra rolled blankets tied to the saddle and slung them over his shoulder, then reached up to lift her from the horse.

He didn't set her on her feet, though. "I'll carry you to Guff's bench," he said, without giving her an opportunity to argue.

She pursed her lips but didn't complain, which made him suspect she was probably more tired than she wanted to let on.

"Okay, but then you'd better come back here to help Tess."

He glanced over and saw that Tess's horse had stopped alongside his big gelding but Tess made no move to climb out of the saddle; she just gazed down at the ground with a nervous kind of look.

"Hang on a minute," he told her. "Just wait there in the saddle while I settle Jo on the bench and then I'll come back to help you down."

"I'm sorry," she said, sounding more disgruntled than apologetic.

"No problem."

He carried Jo along the trail, grateful again for the pale moonlight that filtered through the fringy pines and the bare branches of the aspens.

Windy Lake was a small stream-fed lake, probably no more than two hundred yards across. As a convenient watering hole, it attracted moose and mule deer and even the occasional elk. The water was always ice cold, as he and the others could all attest. That didn't stop him and Brant and Cisco—and Easton, when she could manage to get away—from sneaking out to come up here on summer nights.

Guff always used to keep a small canoe on the shore and they loved any chance to paddle out in the moonlight on July nights and fish for the native rainbow trout and arctic grayling that inhabited it.

Some of his most treasured memories of his teen years centered around trips to this very place.

The trail ended at the lakeshore. He carried Jo to the bench Guff built here, which had been situated in the perfect place to take in the pristine, shimmering lake and the granite mountains surrounding it.

He set Jo on her feet for just a moment so he could

brush pine needles and twigs off the bench. Contrary to what he expected, the bench didn't have months worth of debris covering it, which made him think Easton probably found the occasional chance to make good use of it.

He covered the seat with a plastic garbage bag he had shoved into his pocket earlier in case the bench was damp.

"There you go. Your throne awaits."

She shook her head at his silliness but sat down gingerly, as if the movement pained her. He unrolled one of the blankets and spread it around her shoulders then tucked the other across her lap.

In the moonlight, he saw lines of pain bracketing her mouth and he worried again that this ride into the mountains had been too much for her. Along with the pain, though, he could see undeniable delight at being in this place she loved, one last time.

He supposed sometimes a little pain might be worthwhile in the short-term if it yielded such joy.

As he fussed over the blankets, she reached a thin hand to cover his. "Thank you, my dear. I'm fine now, I promise. Go rescue poor Tess and let me sit here for a moment with my memories."

"Call out if you need help. We won't be far."

"Don't fuss over me," she ordered. "Go help Tess."

Though he was reluctant to leave her here alone, he decided she was safe with the dogs who sat by her side, their ears cocked forward as if listening for any threat.

Back at the trailhead, he found Tess exactly where he had left her, still astride the mare, who was placidly grazing on the last of the autumn grasses.

"I tried to get down," she told him when he emerged from the trees. "Honestly, I did. But my blasted shoe is caught in the stirrups and I couldn't work it loose, no matter how hard I tried. This is so embarrassing."

"I guess that's the price you pay when you go horse-back riding in comfortable nurse's shoes instead of boots."

"If I had known I was going to be roped into this, I would have pulled out my only pair of Tony Lamas for the occasion."

Despite her attempt at a light tone, he caught something in her stiff posture, in the rigid set of her jaw.

This was more than inexperience with horses, he realized as he worked her shoe free of the tight stirrup. Had he really been so overbearing and arrogant in insisting she come along that he refused to see she had a deep aversion to horses?

"I'm sorry I dragged you along."

"It's not all bad." She gazed up at the stars. "It's a lovely night."

"Tell me, how many moonlit rides have you been on into the mountains around Pine Gulch?"

She summoned a smile. "Counting tonight? Exactly one."

He finally worked her shoe free. "Let me help you down," he said.

She released the reins and swiveled her left leg over the saddle horn so she could dismount. The mare moved at just that moment and suddenly his arms were full of warm, delicious curves.

She smelled of vanilla and peaches and much to his dismay, his recalcitrant body stirred to life.

He released her abruptly and she wobbled a little when her feet met solid ground. Out of instinct, he reached to steady her and his hand brushed the curve of her breast when he grabbed her arm. Her gaze flashed to his and in the moonlight, he thought he felt the silky cord of sexual awareness tug between them.

"Okay now?"

"I…think so."

That low, breathy note in her voice had to be his imagination. He was almost certain of it.

He couldn't possibly be attracted to her. Sure, she was still a beautiful woman on the outside, but she was still Tess Claybourne, for heaven's sake.

He noticed she moved a considerable distance away but he wasn't sure if she was avoiding him or the horses. Probably both.

"I'm sorry I dragged you up here," he said again. "I didn't realize how uncomfortable riding would be for you."

She made a face. "It shouldn't be. I'm embarrassed that it is. I grew up around horses—how could I help it in Pine Gulch? Though my family never had them, all my friends did, but I've had an…irrational fear of them since breaking my arm after being bucked off when I was seven."

"And I made you come anyway."

She mustered a smile. "I survived this far. We're halfway done now."

He remembered Jo's words suddenly. *You'll never find a happier soul in all your days. Why, what she's been through would have crushed most women. Not our Tess.*

Jo thought Tess was a survivor. If she weren't, could she be looking at this trip with such calm acceptance, even when she was obviously terrified?

"That's one way of looking at it, I guess."

She didn't meet his gaze. "It's not so bad. After the

way I treated you in high school, I guess I'm surprised you didn't tie me onto the back of your horse and drag me behind you for a few miles."

His gaze narrowed. What game was this? He never, in a million years, would have expected her to refer to her behavior in their shared past, especially when she struck exactly the right note of self-deprecation.

For several awkward seconds, he couldn't think how to respond. Did he shrug it off? Act like he didn't know what she was talking about? Tell her she ought to have *bitch* tattooed across her forehead and he would be happy to pay for it?

"High school seems a long time ago right now," he finally said.

"Surely not so long that you've forgotten."

He couldn't lie to her. "You always made an impression."

Her laughter was short and unamused. "That's one way of phrasing it, I suppose."

"What would you call it?"

"Unconscionable."

At that single, low-voiced word, he studied her in the moonlight—her long-lashed green eyes contrite, that mouth set in a frown, the auburn curls that were a little disheveled from the ride.

How the hell did she do it? Lord knew, he didn't want to be. But against his will, Quinn found himself drawn to this woman who was willing to confront her fears for his aunt's sake, who could make fun of herself, who seemed genuinely contrite about past bad behavior.

He liked her and, worse, was uncomfortably aware of a fierce physical attraction to her soft curves and classical features that seemed so serene and lovely in the moonlight.

He pushed away the insane attraction, just as he pushed away the compelling urge to ask her what he had ever done back then to make her hate him so much. Instead, he did his best to turn the subject away.

"Easton told me about Scott. About the accident."

She shoved her hands in the pocket of her jacket and looked off through the darkened trees toward the direction of the lake. "Did she?"

"She said you had only been married a few months at the time, so most of your marriage you were more of a caregiver than a wife."

"Everybody says that like I made some grand, noble sacrifice."

He didn't want to think so. He much preferred thinking of her as the self-absorbed teenage girl trying to ruin his life.

"What would you consider it?"

"I didn't do anything unusual. He was my husband," she said simply. "I loved him and I took vows. I couldn't just abandon him to some impersonal care center for the rest of his life and blithely go on with my own as if he didn't exist."

Many people he knew wouldn't have blinked twice at responding exactly that way to the situation. Hell, the Tess he thought she had been would have done exactly that.

"Do you regret those years?"

She stared at him for a long moment, her eyes wide with surprise, as if no one had ever asked her that before.

"Sometimes," she admitted, her voice so low he could barely hear it. "I don't regret that I had that extra time with him. I could never regret that. By all rights, he should have died in that accident. A weaker man probably would have. Scott didn't and I have to think God had some purpose in that, something larger than my understanding."

She paused, her expression pensive. "I do regret that we never had the chance to build the life we talked about those first few months of our marriage. Children, a mortgage, a couple of dogs. We missed all that."

Not much of a sacrifice, he thought. He would be quite happy not to have that sort of trouble in his life.

"I'll probably always regret that," she went on. "Unfortunately, I can't change the past. I can only look forward and try to make the best of everything that comes next."

They lapsed into a silence broken only by the horses stamping and snorting behind them and the distant lapping of the water.

She was the first to break the temporary peace. "We'd better go check on Jo, don't you think?"

He jerked his mind away from how very much he wanted to kiss her right this moment, with the moonlight gleaming through the trees and the night creatures singing an accompaniment. "Right. Will you be okay without a flashlight?"

"I'll manage. Just lead the way."

He headed up the trail toward Jo, astonished that his most pressing regret right now was the end of their brief interlude in the moonlight.

* * *

Though Tess loved living in the Mountain West for the people and the scenery and the generally slower pace of life, she had never really considered herself a nature girl.

As a bank manager and accountant, her father hadn't been the sort to take her camping and fishing when she was younger. Later, she'd been too busy, first in college and then taking care of Scott, to find much time to enjoy the backcountry.

But she had to admit she found something serene and peaceful about being here with the glittery stars overhead and that huge glowing moon filtering through the trees and the night alive with sounds and smells.

Well, it would have been serene if she weren't so intensely aware of Quinn walking just ahead of her, moving with long-limbed confidence through the darkness.

The man exuded sensuality. She sighed, wishing she could ignore his effect on her. She disliked the way her heart picked up a beat or two, the little churn of her blood, the way she couldn't seem to keep herself from stealing secret little glances at him as they made their way toward the lake and Jo.

She hadn't missed that moment of awareness in his eyes back there, the heat that suddenly shivered through the air like fireflies on a summer night.

He was attracted to her, though she had a strong sense he found the idea more than appalling.

Her gaze skidded to his powerful shoulders under his denim jacket, to the dark hair that brushed his collar under his Stetson, and her insides trembled.

For a moment there, she had been quite certain he wanted to kiss her, though she couldn't quite fathom it.

How long had it been since she knew the heady, exhilarating impact of desire in a man's eyes? Longer than she cared to remember. The men in town didn't tend to look at her as a woman with the very real and human hunger to be cherished and touched.

In the eyes of most people in Pine Gulch, that woman had been somehow absorbed into the loving, dutiful caretaker, leaving no room for more. Even after Scott's death, people still seemed to see her as a nurturer, not the flirty, sexy, fun-loving Tess she thought might still be buried somewhere deep inside her.

Seeing that heat kindle in his eyes, replacing his typical animosity, had been both flattering and disconcerting and for a moment, she had been mortified at her little spurt of panic, the fear that she had no idea how to respond.

She just needed practice, she assured herself. That's why she was moving to Portland, so she could be around people who saw her as more than just Pine Gulch's version of Mother Teresa.

They walked the short distance through the pines and aspens, their trail lit only by pale moonlight and the glow of a small flashlight he produced from the pocket of his denim jacket. When they reached the lake a few moments later, Tess saw Jo on a bench on the shore, the dogs at her feet. She sat unmoving, so still that for a moment, Tess feared the worst.

But Quinn's boot snapped a twig at that moment and Jo turned her head. Though they were still a few yards away, Tess could see the glow on her features shining through clearly, even in the moonlight. Her friend smiled at them and for one precious instant, she looked younger, happier. Whole.

"There you are. I was afraid the two of you were lost."

Quinn slanted Tess a sidelong look before turning his attention back to his foster mother. "No. I thought you might like a few moments to yourself up here."

Jo smiled at him as she reached a hand out to Tess to draw her down beside her on the bench. When she saw the blankets tucked around Jo's shoulders and across her lap, everything inside her went a little gooey that Quinn had taken such great care to ensure his foster mother's comfort.

"Isn't it lovely, my dear?"

"Breathtaking," Tess assured her, her hand still enclosed around Jo's thin fingers.

They sat like that for a moment with Quinn standing beside them. The moon glowed off the rocky face of the mountains ringing the lake, reflecting in water that seethed and bubbled as if it was some sort of hot springs. After several moments of watching it, Tess realized the percolating effect was achieved by dozens of fish rising to the surface for night-flying insects.

"It's enchanting," she said to Jo, squeezing her fingers. She didn't add that this moment, this shared beauty, was almost worth that miserable horseback ride up the mountainside.

"This is such a gift. I cannot tell you how deeply it touches me. I have missed these mountains so much these past weeks while I've been stuck at home. Thank you both so very much."

Jo's smile was wide and genuine but Tess didn't miss the lines of pain beneath it that radiated from her mouth.

Quinn must have noticed them as well. "I'd love to stay here longer," he said after a moment, "but we had better get you back. Tess has other patients."

Jo nodded, a little sadly, Tess thought. A lump rose in her throat as the other woman rose, her face tilted to the huge full moon. Jo closed her eyes, inhaled a deep breath of mountain air, then let it out slowly before turning back to Quinn.

"I'm ready."

Her chest felt achy and tight with unshed tears watching Jo say this private goodbye to a place she loved. It didn't help her emotions at all when Quinn carefully and tenderly scooped Jo into his arms and carried her back toward the waiting horses.

She pushed back the tears as she awkwardly mounted her horse, knowing Jo wouldn't welcome them at all. The older woman accepted her impending passing with grace and acceptance, something Tess could only wish on all her patients.

The ride down was slightly easier than the way up had been, though she wouldn't have expected it. In her limited experience on the back of a horse, gravity hadn't always been her friend.

Perhaps she was a tiny bit more loose and relaxed than she had been on the way up. At least she didn't grip the reins quite so tightly and her body seemed to more readily pick up the rhythm of the horse's gait.

She had heard somewhere that horses were sensitive creatures who picked up on those sorts of things like anxiety and apprehension. Maybe the little mare was just giving her the benefit of the doubt.

As she had on the way up the trail, she rode in the rear of their little group, behind the two black and white dogs and Quinn and Jo, which gave her the opportunity to watch his gentle solicitude toward her.

She found something unbearably sweet—disarming, even—at the sight of his tender care, such a vivid contrast to his reputation as a ruthless businessman who had built his vast shipping company from the ground up.

That treacherous softness fluttered inside her. Even after she forced herself to look away—to focus instead on the rare beauty of the night settling in more deeply across the mountainside—she couldn't ignore that tangled mix of fierce attraction and dawning respect.

As they descended the trail, Winder Ranch came into view, sprawling and solid in the night.

"Home," Jo said in a sleepy-sounding voice that carried across the darkness.

"We're nearly there," he assured her.

When they arrived at the ranch house, Quinn dismounted and then reached for Jo, who winced with the movement.

Worry spasmed across his handsome features but she watched him quickly conceal it from Jo. "Tess, do you mind holding the horses for a few moments while I carry Jo inside and settle her back in her bedroom?"

This time, she was pleased that she could dismount on her own. "Of course not," she answered as her feet hit the dirt.

"Thank you. I'll trade places with you in a few moments so that you can get Jo settled for bed while I take care of the horses."

"Good plan."

She gave him a hesitant smile and was a little astonished when he returned it. Something significant had changed between them as a result of one simple horseback ride into the mountains. They were working together, a team, at least for the moment. He seemed warmer, more approachable. Less antagonistic.

They hadn't really cleared any air between them, other than those few moments she had tried to offer an oblique apology for their history. But she wanted to think perhaps he might eventually come to accept that she had become a better person.

Chapter Seven

After Quinn carried Jo inside, Tess stood patting the mare, savoring the night before she went inside to take care of Jo's medical needs. Quiet moments of reflection were a rare commodity in her world.

She had gotten out of the habit when she had genuinely had no time to spare with all of Scott's medical needs. Perhaps she needed to work at meditation when she moved to Portland, she thought. Maybe yoga or tai chi.

She was considering her options and talking softly to the horses when Quinn hurried down the porch steps a few moments later.

"How's Jo?"

"Ready for pain meds, I think, but she's not complaining."

"You gave her a great gift tonight, Quinn."

He smiled a little. "I hope so. She loves the mountains. I have to admit, I do as well. I forget that sometimes. Seattle is beautiful with the water and the volcanic mountains but it's not the same as home."

"Is it? Home, I mean?"

"Always."

He spoke with no trace of hesitation and she wondered again at the circumstances that had led him to Winder Ranch. Those rumors about his violent past swirled through her memory and she quickly dismissed them as ridiculous.

"I'm sorry. Let me take the horses." He reached for the reins of both horses and as she handed them over, their hands brushed.

He flashed her a quick look and grabbed her fingers with his other hand. "Your fingers are freezing!"

"I should have worn gloves."

"I should have thought to get you some before we left." He paused. "This was a crazy idea, wasn't it? I apologize again for dragging you up there."

"Not a crazy idea at all," she insisted. "Jo loved it."

"She's half-asleep in there and I know she's in pain but she's also happier than I've seen her since I arrived."

She smiled at him, intensely conscious of the hard strength of his hand still curled around her fingers. Her hands might still be cold from the night air but they were just about the only thing not heating up right about now.

He gazed at her mouth for several long seconds, his eyes silvery-blue in the moonlight, and for one effervescent moment, she thought again that he might kiss her. He even angled his head ever so slightly and her gaze tangled with his.

Her pulse seemed abnormally loud in her ears and her insides jumped and fluttered like a baby bird trying its first awkward flight.

He eased forward slightly and her body instinctively rose to meet his. She caught her breath, waiting for the brush of his mouth against hers, but he suddenly jerked back, his expression thunderstruck.

Tess blinked as if awakening from a long, lovely nap as cold reality splashed over her. Of course he wouldn't kiss her. He despised her, with very good reason.

With ruthless determination, she shoved down the disappointment and ridiculous sense of hurt shivering through her. So what if he found the idea of kissing her so abhorrent? She didn't have time for this anyway. She was supposed to be working, not going for moonlit rides and sharing confidences in the dark and fantasizing about finally kissing her teenage crush.

Since he now held the horses' reins, she shoved her hands in the pocket of her jacket to hide their trembling and forced her voice to sound cool and unaffected.

"I'd better go take care of Jo's meds."

"Right." He continued to watch her out of those seductive but veiled eyes.

"Um, good night, if I don't see you again before I leave."

"Good night."

She hurried up the porch steps, feeling the heat of his gaze following her. Inside, she closed the door and leaned against it for just a moment, willing her heart to settle down once more.

Blast the man for stirring up all these hormones she tried so hard to keep contained. She *so* did not want to be attracted to Quinn. What a colossal waste of energy on her part. Oh, he might have softened toward her a little in the course of their ride with Jo, but she couldn't delude herself into thinking he was willing to forgive and forget everything she had done to him years ago.

She had work to do, she reminded herself. People who needed her. She didn't have time to be obsessing over the past or the person she used to be or a man like Quinn Southerland, who could never see her as anything else.

She did her best the rest of the night to focus on her patients and not on the little thrum of desire she hadn't been able to shake since that almost-kiss with Quinn.

Still, she approached Winder Ranch for her midnight check on Jo with a certain amount of trepidation. To her relief, when she unlocked the door with the key Easton had given her and walked inside, the house was dark. Quinn was nowhere in sight, but she could still sense his presence in the house.

Jo didn't stir when Tess entered her room, which worried her for a moment until she saw the steady rise and fall of the blankets by the glow of the small light in the attached bathroom that Jo and Easton left on for the hospice nurses.

The ride up to the lake must have completely exhausted her. She didn't even wake when Tess checked her vitals and gave her medicine through the central IV line that had been placed after her last hospitalization.

When she was done with the visit, she closed the door quietly behind her and turned to go, then became aware that someone else was in the darkened hallway. Her heart gave a quick, hard kick, then she realized it was Easton.

She wasn't sure if that sensation coursing through her was more disappointment or relief.

"I hope I didn't wake you," Tess said.

The other woman's sleek blond ponytail moved as she shook her head. "I've still got some pesky accounts to finish. I was in the office working on the computer and heard the door open."

"I tried to be quiet. Sorry about that." She smiled at her friend. "But then, Jo didn't even wake up so I couldn't have been *too* loud."

"You weren't. I'm just restless tonight."

"I'm sorry."

Easton shrugged. "It sometimes knocks me on my butt if I think about what things will be like in a month or so. I'm trying to get as much done now on ranch paperwork so I have time to…to grieve."

Tess placed a comforting hand on her arm and Easton smiled, making a visible effort to push away her sadness. "Quinn told me about your adventure tonight," she said.

Tess made a rueful face. "I'm nowhere near the horsewoman you are. I felt like an idiot up there, but at least I didn't fall off."

"Jo was so happy when I checked on her earlier. I haven't seen her like that in a long time."

"Then I suppose my mortification was all for a good cause."

Easton laughed a little but her laughter quickly faded. "It won't be much longer, will it?"

Tess's heart ached at the question but she didn't pretend to misunderstand. "A week, maybe a little more. You know I can't say exactly."

Her friend's blue eyes filled with a sorrow that was

raw and real. "I don't want to lose her, Tess. I'm not ready. What will I do?"

Tess set her bag on the floor and hurried forward to pull Easton into her arms. She knew that ache, that deep, gnawing fear and loss.

"You'll go on. That's all you can do. All any of us can do."

"First my parents, then Guff and now Jo. I can't bear it. She's all I have left."

"I know, sweetheart."

Easton didn't cry aloud, though Tess could feel the quiet shuddering of her shoulders. After a moment, the other woman pulled away.

"I'm sorry. I'm just tired."

"You need to sleep, honey. Everything will seem a little better in the morning, I promise. Midnight is the time when our fears all grow stronger and more vicious."

Easton drew in a heavy breath, then stepped away, swiping at her eyes. "Brant called from Germany earlier. He's hoping to get a flight any time now."

She remembered Brant Western as a tall, serious-minded boy who had always seemed an odd fit to be best friends with both Quinn, the rebellious kid with the surly attitude, and Cisco Del Norte, the wild, slightly dangerous troublemaker.

"Jo will be thrilled to have him home. What about Cisco?"

Easton's mouth compressed into a tight line and she focused on a spot somewhere over Tess's shoulder. "No word yet. We think he's somewhere in El Salvador but we can't seem to find anything out for sure. He's moving around a lot. Seems like everywhere we try, we just keep

missing him by a day or even a few hours. It's so aggravating. Quinn has his assistant in Seattle trying to pull
some strings with the embassy down there to find him."

"I hope it doesn't take much longer."

Easton nodded, her features troubled. "Even if we
find him, there's no guarantee he can make it back in
time. Quinn has promised to send a plane down to bring
him home, even if he's in the middle of the jungle, but
we have to find him first."

Her stomach gave a strange little quiver at the idea
of Quinn having planes at his disposal.

"I'll keep my fingers crossed," she said, then picked
up her bag and headed for the front door. Easton
followed to let her out.

"Get some rest, honey," she said again. "I'll be back
for the next round of meds around three. You'd better
be asleep when I get back!"

"Yes, Nurse Ratched."

"I mean it."

Easton smiled a little, even past the lingering sadness
in her eyes. "Thanks, Tess. For everything."

"Go to sleep," she ordered again, then walked out
into the night, with that same curious mix of relief and
disappointment that she had avoided Quinn, at least for
a few more hours.

He awoke to the sound of a door snicking softly
closed and the dimmer switch in the bathroom being
turned up just enough to jar him out of dreams he had
no business entertaining.

In a rather surreal paradigm shift, he went from
dreaming about a heated embrace on a warm blanket

under starry skies near the lake to the stark reality of a sickroom, where his foster mother lay dying.

Oddly, the same woman appeared in both scenes. Tess stepped out of the bathroom, looking brisk and professional in her flowered surgical scrubs.

He feigned sleep and watched her through his lashes as she donned a pair of latex-free gloves.

He could pinpoint the instant she saw him sprawled in the recliner, purportedly asleep. Her steps faltered and she froze.

Probably the decent thing would be to open his eyes and go through the motions of pretending to awaken. But he wasn't always crazy about doing the decent thing. Instead, he gave a heavy-sounding breath and continued to spy on her under his lashes.

She gazed at him for several seconds as if trying to ascertain his level of sleep, then she finally turned away from him and back to her patient with a small, barely perceptible sigh he wondered about.

For the next few minutes, he watched her draw medicine out into syringes, then she quietly began checking Jo's blood pressure and temperature.

Though her movements were slow and careful, Jo still opened her eyes when Tess put the blood pressure cuff on her leg.

"I'm so sorry to wake you. I wish I didn't have to," Tess murmured.

"Oh, poof," Jo whispered back. "Don't you worry for a single moment about doing your job."

"How is your pain level?"

Jo was silent. "I'm not going to tell you," she finally said. "You'll just write it down in your little chart and the next thing I know, Jake Dalton will be increasing my meds and I'll be so drugged out I won't be able to think straight. My Brant is coming home. Should be any day now."

As Jo whispered to her, Tess continued to slant careful looks in his direction.

"Easton told me earlier that he was on his way," she said in an undertone.

"They'll be good for Easton. The four of them, why, they were thicker than thieves. I can't tell you how glad I am they'll still have each other."

Quinn swallowed hard, hating this whole situation all over again.

Tess smiled, relentlessly cheerful. "It's a blessing, all right. For all of them and especially for your peace of mind."

He listened to their quiet conversation as Tess continued to take care of Jo's medical needs. He was still trying to figure out how much of her demeanor he was buying. She seemed to be everything that was patient and calm, a serene island in the middle of a stormy emotional mess. Was it truly possible that this dramatic change in her could be genuine?

He supposed he was a cynical bastard but he couldn't quite believe it. This could all be one big show she was putting on. He had only been here a few days. If he stuck around long enough, she was likely to revert to her true colors.

On the other hand, people could change. He was living testimony to that. He was worlds away from the bitter, hot-tempered punk he'd been when he arrived at the Winders' doorstep after a year in foster care and the misery that came before.

He pushed away the past, preferring instead to focus on today.

Tess finished with Jo a few moments later. After fluffing her pillow and tucking the blankets up around her, she dimmed the light in the bathroom again and moved quietly toward the door out into the hallway.

He rose and followed her, careful not to disturb Jo, who seemed to have easily slipped into sleep again.

"I'll walk you out," he said, his voice low, just as she reached the door.

She whirled and splayed a hand across her chest. She glared at him as she moved out of the room to the hallway. He followed her and closed the door behind him.

"Don't do that! That's the second time you've nearly scared the life out of me. How long have you been awake?"

"Not long. Here, let me help you with your coat."

He took it off the chair in the hallway where she had tossed it and stood behind her. Her scent teased him, that delectable peach and vanilla, that somehow seemed sweet and sultry at the same time, like a hot Southern night.

She paused for a moment, then extended her arm through the sleeve. "Thank you," she said and he wondered if he was imagining the slightly husky note to her voice.

"You're welcome."

"You really don't need to walk me out, though. I'm sure I can find the way to my car by myself."

"I could use the fresh air, to be honest with you."

She looked as if she wanted to argue but she only shrugged and turned toward the door. He held it open for her and again smelled that seductive scent as she moved past him on her way out.

The scent seemed to curl through him, twisting and tugging an unwelcome response out of him, which he did his best to ignore as they walked out into the night.

The moon hung huge over the western mountains now, the stars a bright glitter out here unlike anything to be found in the city.

The October night wasn't just cool now in the early morning hours, it was downright cold. This time of year, temperatures in these high mountain valleys could show a wide range in the course of a single day. Nights were invariably cool, even in summer. In spring and fall, the temperature dropped quickly once the sun went down.

His morning spent in the garden soaking up sunshine with Jo seemed only another distant memory.

"Gorgeous night, isn't it?" Tess said. "I don't ever get tired of the view out here."

He nodded. "I've lived without it since I left Cold Creek Canyon, but something about it stays inside me even when I'm back in Seattle."

She smiled a little. "I know I'm going to miss these mountains when I move to Portland in a few weeks."

"What's in Portland?" he asked, curious as to why she would pick up and leave after her lifetime spent here.

"A pretty good basketball team," she answered. "Lots of trees and flowers. Nice people, from what I hear."

"You know what I mean. Why are you leaving?"

She was silent for a moment, the only sound the wind whispering through the trees. "A whole truckload of reasons. Mostly, I guess, because I'm ready for a new start."

He could understand that. He had sought the same

thing in the Air Force after leaving Pine Gulch, hadn't he? A place where no one knew his history in the foster-care system or as the rough-edged punk who had found a home here with Jo and Guff.

"Will you be doing the same thing? Providing end-of-life care?"

She smiled and in the moonlight, she looked fresh and lovely and very much like the teenage cheerleader who had tangled the hormones of every boy who walked the halls of Pine Gulch High School.

"Just the opposite, actually. I took a job in labor and delivery at one of the Portland hospitals."

"Bringing life into the world instead of comforting those who are leaving it. There's a certain symmetry to that."

"I think so, too. It's all part of my brand-new start."

"I suppose everybody could use that once in a while."

"True enough," she murmured, with an unreadable look in her eyes.

"Will you miss this?"

"Pine Gulch?"

"I was thinking more of the work you do. You seem…very good at it. Do you give this same level to all your patients as you have to Jo?"

She looked startled at the question, though he wasn't sure if was because she had never thought about it before or that she was surprised he had noticed.

"I try. Everyone deserves to spend his or her last days with dignity and respect. But Jo is special. I can't deny that. She used to give me piano lessons when I was young and I've always adored her."

Now it was his turn to be surprised. Jo taught piano

lessons for many years to most of the young people in Pine Gulch but he had never realized Tess had once had the privilege of being one of her students.

"Do you still play?"

She laughed. "I hardly played then. I was awful. Probably the worst student Jo ever had, though she tried her best, believe me. But yes, I still play a little. I enjoy it much more as an adult than I did when I was ten."

She paused for a moment, then gave a rueful smile. "When he was…upset or having a bad day, Scott used to enjoy when I would play for him. It calmed him. I've had more practice than I ever expected over the years."

"You should play for Jo sometime when you come out to the house. She gets a real kick out of hearing her old students play. Especially the hard ones."

"Maybe. I'm worried her hearing is a little too fragile for my fumbling attempts." She smiled. "What about you? Did Jo give you lessons after you moved here?"

He gave a short laugh at the memory. "She tried. I'm sure I could have taught you a thing or two about being difficult."

"I don't doubt that for a moment," she murmured.

She gazed at him for a moment, then she shifted her gaze up and he could swear he saw a million constellations reflected in her eyes.

"Look!" she exclaimed. "A shooting star, right over the top of Windy Peak. Quick, make a wish."

He tilted his neck to look in the direction she pointed. "Probably just a satellite."

She glared at him. "Don't ruin it. I'm making a wish anyway."

With her eyes screwed closed, she pursed her mouth

in concentration. "There," she said after a moment. "That should do it."

She opened her eyes and smiled softly at him and he forgot all about the cold night air. All he could focus on was that smile, that mouth, and the sudden wild hunger inside him to taste it.

"What did you wish?" he asked, a gruff note to his voice.

She made a face. "If I tell you, it won't come true. Don't you know anything about wishes?"

Right now, he could tell her a thing or two about wanting something he shouldn't. That sensuous heat wrapped tighter around his insides. "I know enough. I know sometimes wishes can be completely ridiculous and make no sense. For instance, right now, I wish I could kiss you. Don't ask me why. I don't even like you."

Her eyes looked huge and green in her delicate face as she stared at him. "Okay," she said, her voice breathy.

"Okay, I can kiss you? Or, okay, you won't ask why I want to?"

She let out a ragged-sounding breath. "Either. Both."

He didn't need much more of an invitation than that. Without allowing himself to stop and think through the insanity of kissing a woman he had detested twenty-four hours earlier, Quinn stepped forward and covered her mouth with his.

Chapter Eight

She gave a little gasp of shock but her mouth was warm and inviting in the cold air and he was vaguely aware through the haze of his own desire that she didn't pull away, as he might have expected.

Instead, she wrapped her arm around his waist and leaned into his kiss for more.

A low clamor in his brain warned him this was a crazy idea, that he would have a much harder time keeping a safe distance between them after he had known the silky softness of her mouth, but he ignored it.

How could he possibly step away now, when she tasted like coffee and peaches and Tess, a delectable combination that sizzled through him like heat lightning?

Her lips parted slightly, all the invitation he needed to deepen the kiss. She moaned a little against his mouth and he could feel the tremble of her body against him, the confused desire in the slide of her tongue against his.

The night disappeared until it was only the two of them, until he was lost in the unexpected hunger for this woman in his arms. Her kiss offered solace and surrender, a chance to put away for a moment his sadness and embrace the wonder of life in all its tragedy and glory.

He lost track of time there in the moonlight. He forgot about Jo and about his efforts to find his recalcitrant foster brother and his worries for Easton. He especially refused to let himself remember all the reasons he shouldn't be kissing her—how, as he'd told her, he wasn't even sure he liked her, how he still didn't trust that she wasn't hiding a knife behind her back, ready to gut him with it at the first chance.

The only thing that mattered for this instant was Tess and how very perfect she felt in his arms, with her mouth eager and warm against his.

A coyote howled from far off in the distance, long and mournful. He heard it on the edge of his consciousness but he knew the instant the spell between them shattered and Tess returned to reality. In the space between one ragged breath and the next, she went from kissing him with heat and passion to freezing in his arms like Windy Lake in a January blizzard.

Her arms fluttered away from around his neck and he sensed she would have backed farther away from him if she hadn't been pressed up against her car door.

Though he wanted nothing more than to crush her to him again and slide into that stunning heat once more, he forced himself to step back to give them both a little necessary space.

Her breathing was as rough and quick as his own and he could see the rapid rise and fall of her chest.

Despite the chill in the air, the night seemed to wrap around them in a sultry embrace. From the trees whispering in the wind to the carpet of stars overhead, they seemed alone here in the darkness.

Part of him wanted to step toward her and sweep her into his arms again, but shock and dismay began to seep through his desire. What kind of magic did she wield against him that he could so easily succumb to his attraction and kiss her, despite all his best instincts?

He shouldn't have done it. In the first place, their relationship was a tangled mess and had been for years. Sure, she had been great with Jo tonight and he had been grateful for her help on the horseback ride into the mountains. But one night couldn't completely transform so much animosity into fuzzy warmth.

In the second place, he had enough on his plate right now. His emotions were scraped raw by Jo's condition. He had nothing left inside to give anything else right now, especially not an unwanted attraction to Tess.

Maybe that's why he had kissed her. He needed the distraction, a few moments of oblivion. Either way, it had been a monumentally stupid impulse, one he was quite certain he would come to regret the moment she climbed into her little sedan and drove down Cold Creek Canyon.

She continued to gaze at him out of those huge green eyes, as if she expected him to say something. He would be damned if he would apologize for kissing her. Not when she had responded with such fierce enthusiasm.

He had to say something, though. He scrambled for words and said the first thing that came to his head.

"If I had known you were such an enthusiastic kisser, I wouldn't have worked so hard to fight you off in high school."

The moment he said the words, he wished he could call them back. The comment had been unnecessarily cruel and made him sound like an ass. Beyond that, he didn't like revealing he remembered anything that had happened in their long-ago past. Apparently she still tended to bring out the worst in him.

He couldn't be certain in the darkness but he thought she paled a little. She grabbed her car door and yanked it open.

"That's funny," she retorted. "If I had known you would turn out to be such a jerk, I wouldn't have spent a moment since you returned to Pine Gulch regretting the way I treated you back then."

He deserved that, he supposed. *Now* he wanted to apologize—for his words at least, not the kiss—but the words seemed to clog in his throat.

She slid into her driver's seat, avoiding his gaze. "It would probably be better for both our sakes if we just pretended the past few moments never happened."

He raised an eyebrow. "You think you can do that? Because I'm not at all sure I have that much imagination."

She cranked the key in her ignition with just a little more force than strictly necessary and he felt a moment's pity that she was taking out her anger against him on her hapless engine.

"Absolutely," she snapped. "It shouldn't be hard at all. Especially since I'm sorry to report the reality didn't come close to measuring up to all my ridiculous teenage fantasies about what it might be like to kiss the bad boy of Cold Creek."

Before he could come up with any kind of re-joinder—sharp or otherwise—she thrust her car into gear and shot around the circular driveway.

He stared after her, wondering why the cold night only now seemed to pierce the haze of desire still wrapped around him.

Her words about teenage fantasies seemed to echo through his head. He supposed on some level, he must have known she had wanted to kiss him all those years ago. She had tried it, after all. He could still remember that day in the empty algebra classroom when he had been so furious with her over the false cheating allegations and then she had made everything much worse by thinking she could reel him in with a few flirtatious words.

He had always assumed her fleeting interest in him, her attempts to draw his attention, were only a spoiled fit of pique that he didn't fall at her feet like every other boy in school. Now he had to wonder if there might have been something more to it.

Trust him to make a mess out of everything, as usual. She had been kind to Jo and he had responded by taking completely inappropriate advantage. Then he had com-pounded his sins by making a stupid, mocking comment for no good reason.

She was furious with him, and she had every right to be, but he couldn't help thinking it was probably better this way. He didn't like having these soft, warm feelings for her.

Better to remember her as that manipulative little

cheerleader looking so sweet-faced and innocent as she lied through her teeth to their history teacher and the principal than as the gentle caregiver who could suppress her own fears about horseback riding to help a dying woman find a little peace.

Tess waited until she drove under the arch at the entrance to Winder Ranch and had turned back onto the main Cold Creek road, out of view of the ranch house, before pulling her car over to the side and shifting into Park with hands that still trembled.

She was such an idiot.

Her face burned and she covered her hot cheeks with her hands.

She couldn't believe her response to him, that she had kissed him with such heat and enthusiasm. The moment his mouth touched hers, she had tossed every ounce of good sense she possessed into the air and had fallen into his kiss like some love-starved teenage girl with a fierce crush.

Oh, mercy. What must he think of her?

Probably that she was a love-starved thirty-two-year-old who hadn't known a man's touch in more years than she cared to remember.

How had she forgotten that incredible rush of sensations churning through her body? The delicious heat and lassitude that turned her brain to mush and her bones to rubber?

She had nearly burst into tears at how absolutely perfect it had felt to have his arms around her, his mouth sure and confident on hers. Wouldn't *that* have been humiliating? Thank the Lord she at least had retained some tiny modicum of dignity. But she had wanted to lose herself inside that kiss, to become so tangled up in him that she could forget the hundreds of reasons she shouldn't be kissing Quinn Southerland on a cold October night outside Winder Ranch.

If I had known you were such an enthusiastic kisser, I wouldn't have worked so hard to fight you off in high school.

His words seemed to echo through her car and she wanted to sink through the floorboards in complete mortification.

What was she thinking? Quinn Southerland, for heaven's sake! The man despised her, rightfully so. If she wanted to jump feet-first into the whole sexual attraction thing, shouldn't she *try* to have the sense God gave a goose and pick somebody who could at least stand to be in the same room with her?

The unpalatable truth was, she hadn't been thinking at all. From the first instant his mouth had touched hers with such stunning impact, she felt like that shooting star she had wished upon, bursting through the atmosphere.

She had been rocked to her core by the wild onrush of sensations, his hands sure and masculine, his rough, late-evening shadow against her skin, his scent—of sleepy male and the faint lingering hint of some expensive aftershave—subtle and sexy at the same time.

To her great shame, she had wanted to forget everything sensible and sound and just surrender to the heat of his kiss. Who knew how long she would have let him continue things if she hadn't heard the lonely sound of a coyote?

Blast the man. She had everything planned out so perfectly. Her new job, relocating to Portland. It wasn't fair that he should come back now and stir up her insides like a tornado touching down. She didn't need this sort of complication just as she was finally on the brink of moving on with her life.

She scrubbed at her cheeks for another moment, then dropped her hands and took a deep, cleansing breath. The tragic truth was, he wouldn't be around much longer and she wouldn't have to deal with him. Jo was clinging by her fingernails but she couldn't hold on much longer. When she passed, Quinn would return to Seattle and she would be starting her new life.

For a few weeks, she would just have to do her best to deal with this insane reaction, to conceal it from him.

He didn't like her and she would be damned if she would pant after him like she was still that teenage girl with a crush.

"Thanks a million for taking a look at the Beast," Easton said. "I really didn't want to have to haul it to the repair place in town."

Four days after his startling encounter with Tess, Quinn stood with his hands inside Easton's temperamental tractor, trying to replace the clutch. "No problem," he answered. "It's good to know I can still find my way around the insides of a John Deere."

"If Southerland Shipping ever hits the skids, you can always come back home and be my grease monkey."

He grinned. "It's always good to have options, isn't it?"

She returned his smile, but it faded quickly. "Guff wanted you to stay and do just that, didn't he? You could always find your way around any kind of combustion engine."

True enough. He never minded other ranch work—roundup and moving the cattle and even hauling hay. But he had always been happiest when he was up to his elbows in grease, tinkering with this or that machine.

"Remember that old '66 Chevy pickup truck you used to work on? The blue one with the white top and all those curves?"

"Oh, yeah. She was a sweet ride. I imagine Cisco drove her into the ground after I left for the Air Force."

Something strange flashed in her mind for a moment, before she blinked it away. "You could have stayed. You would have been more than welcome," Easton said after a moment. "But I knew all along you never would."

He raised an eyebrow. Had he been so transparent? "Pine Gulch is a nice place and I love the ranch. Why were you so certain I wouldn't stick around? I might have been happy running a little place of my own nearby."

She shook her head. "Not you. Brant, maybe. He loves his ranch, though you would have to use that crowbar in the toolbox over there to get him to admit it. But you and Cisco had wanderlust running through your veins even when we were kids."

Maybe Cisco, Quinn thought. He had always talked about all the places he wanted to see when he left Idaho. Sun-drenched beaches and glittering cities and beautiful, exotic women who would drop their clothes if you so much as smiled at them.

That had been Francisco Del Norte's teenage dream. Quinn had no idea how close he had come to reaching it, since the man was wickedly skillful at evading any questions about his wandering life.

Quinn had his suspicions about what Cisco might be involved with, but he preferred to keep them to himself, especially around Easton. While she might love him and Brant like brothers, he had always sensed her feelings for Cisco were far different.

"I haven't wandered that far," he protested, instead of dwelling on Cisco and his suitcase full of secrets. "Not since I left the Air Force, anyway. I've been settled in Seattle for eight years now."

"Your dreams were always bigger than a little town like Pine Gulch could hold. I think deep down, Guff and Jo knew that, even if they were disappointed you didn't come home after you were discharged."

"They didn't need me here. They always had you to run the ranch." He sent her a careful look. "I always figured you were just fine with that. Was I wrong? You left for a while there, but you came back."

She had that strange look in her eyes again when he mentioned the eight months she had moved away from the ranch after Guff died. She didn't like to talk about it much, other than to say she had needed a change for a while. He supposed, like Cisco, she had her share of secrets, too.

"Yes. I came back," she said.

"Do you regret that?"

She raised her eyebrows. "You mean do I feel stuck here while the rest of you went off and conquered the world?"

He made a face. "I haven't *completely* conquered it. Still have a ways to go there but I'm working on it."

She smiled, though her expression was pensive. "I can't deny that sometimes I wonder if there's something more out there for me than a cattle ranch in Pine Gulch,

Idaho. But I'm happy here, for the most part. I can't bear the thought of selling the ranch and leaving. Where would I go?"

"You could always come to Seattle. The company could always use somebody with your organizational skills."

"That world's not for me. You know that. I'm happy here."

Even as she said it, he caught the wistful note in her voice and he wondered at it. It wouldn't be easy to just pick up and make a new start somewhere. As had been the case more often than he cared to admit, he couldn't help thinking about Tess. In a few weeks, she was off to make a new start somewhere away from Pine Gulch.

As he worked on the clutch, his mind replayed that stunning kiss a few days earlier: the taste of her, like coffee and cinnamon, the sweet scent of her surrounding him, the imprint of her soft curves burning through layers of clothing.

He could go for long stretches of time without thinking about it as he went about the routine of visiting with Jo, helping Easton with odd jobs and trying to run Southerland Shipping from hundreds of miles away.

But then something would spark a memory and he would find himself once more caught up in reliving every moment of that heated embrace.

He let out a breath, grateful he had seen Tess just a few times since, when she came out to take care of Jo—and then only briefly, in the buffering presence of Easton or Jo. He had wanted to apologize but hadn't been alone with her to do it and hadn't wanted to bring up the kiss in the presence of either of the other women.

That hadn't stopped him from obsessing more than he should have about her when she wasn't around, wondering which was the real Tess—the selfish girl he remembered or the soft, caring woman she appeared to be now.

The sound of an approaching vehicle drew his attention from either the mystery of Tess or the tractor's insides.

"Looks like company." Through the wide doors of the ranch's equipment shed, he watched a small white SUV approach the house. "Isn't it too early in the afternoon for any caregivers? The nurse was just here."

Easton followed his gaze outside. "I don't recognize the vehicle. Maybe it's one of Jo's friends."

They watched for a moment from their vantage point of a hundred yards away as the door opened, then a tall, brown-haired man in uniform stepped out.

"Brant!" Easton exclaimed, her delicate features alight with joy.

With a resounding thud that echoed through the building, she dropped the wrench to the concrete equipment shed floor and ran full-tilt toward the new arrival.

Quinn followed at an easier pace and arrived just as Brant Western scooped East into his arms for a tight hug.

"I'll get grease all over your pretty uniform," she warned.

"I don't care. You are a sight, Blondie."

"Back at you." She kissed his cheek and Quinn watched her dash tears away with a surreptitious finger swipe. He remembered again the little tow-headed preteen who used to follow them around everywhere.

He couldn't believe her parents had let them drag her along on all their adventures but she had always been a plucky little thing and they had all adored her.

After another tight hug, Brant set her down, then turned to Quinn with a long, considering glance.

"Look at you. A few days back on the ranch and Easton has you doing all the grunt work."

He looked down at the oil and grime that covered his shirt. "I don't mind getting my hands a little dirty."

"You never did." Brant smiled, though his eyes were red-rimmed with exhaustion. He looked not just fatigued but emotionally wrung-out.

Quinn considered Brant and Cisco his best friends, his brothers in every way that mattered. And though they had never been particularly demonstrative with each other, he was compelled now to step forward and pound the other man's back.

"Welcome home, Major."

"Thanks, man."

"Now I'm the one who's going to get grease all over your uniform."

"It will wash." Brant stepped away and Quinn was happy to see he seemed a little brighter, not quite as utterly exhausted. "On the flight over, I was trying to remember how long it's been since we've been together like this."

"Four years ago January," Easton said promptly.

Quinn combed through his memory bank and realized that must have been when Guff had died of a heart attack that had shocked all of them. By some miracle, they had all made it back from the various corners of the world for his funeral.

"Too damn long, that's for sure," he said.

Brant smiled for a moment but quickly sobered. "Like the last one, I wish this reunion could be under happier circumstances. How is she?"

"Eager to see you." Easton slipped her arm through his. "She'll be so happy you could make it home."

"I can't stay long. I was able to swing only a week. I'll have my regular leave in January and will have a couple more weeks home then if I can make it back."

Jo wouldn't be around for that and all of them knew it.

Easton forced a smile. "A day or a week, it won't matter to Jo. She'll just be so happy she had a chance to see you one last time. Come on, I'll take you inside. I want to see her face when she gets a load of you."

"You two go ahead," Quinn said. "I'm almost done out here. Since I'm already dirty, think I'll finish up out here first and come inside in a few."

Brant and Easton both nodded and headed for the house while Quinn returned to the tractor. A few minutes later, he was just tightening the last nut on the job when he heard the front door to the house bang shut.

"Quinn! Come quick!"

He jerked his gaze toward the ranch house at the urgency in Easton's voice and his blood ran cold.

He dropped the wrench and raced toward the house. Not yet, he prayed as he ran. Not when Brant had only just arrived at Winder Ranch and when his people hadn't managed to find Cisco yet.

His heart pounded frantically as he thrust open the door to Jo's room. The IV pump was beeping and the alarm was going off on the oxygen saturation monitor.

He frowned. Jo was lying against her pillow but wild

relief pulsed through him that her eyes were open and alert, though her features were pale and drawn.

Just now, Easton looked in worse shape than Jo. She stood by the bedside, the phone in her hand.

"I don't care what you say. I'm calling Dr. Dalton. You were unconscious!"

"All this bother and fuss," Jo muttered. "You're making me feel like a foolish old woman."

Despite her effort to downplay her condition, he could see the concern in the expressions of both Brant and Easton.

"She was out cold for five solid minutes," Easton explained to Quinn. "She was hugging Brant one moment, then she fell back against her pillows the next and wouldn't wake up no matter what we tried."

"I should have called to let you know I was on my way." Brant's voice was tight with self-disgust. "It wasn't right to rush in like that and surprise you."

"I wasn't expecting you today, that's all," Jo insisted. "Maybe I got a little excited but I'm fine now."

Despite her protestations, Jo was as pale as her pillow.

"The clinic's line is busy. I'm calling Tess," Easton declared and walked from the room to make the call.

"Tess?" Brant asked.

Just when his heart rate started to slow from the adrenaline rush, simply the mention of Tess's name kicked it right back up again.

"Tess Claybourne. Used to be Jamison. She's one of the hospice nurses."

The best one, he had to admit. After several days here, he knew all three of the home-care nurses who took turns seeing to Jo. They were all good caregivers and compassionate women but as tough as it was for him to swallow, Tess had a knack for easing Jo's worst moments and calming everybody else in the house.

Brant's blue eyes widened. "Tess Jamison. Pom-pom Tess? Homecoming queen? That Tess?"

Okay, already. "Yeah. That Tess."

"You're yanking my chain."

"Not this time." He couldn't keep the grimness out of his voice.

"She still hotter than a two-dollar pistol?"

"Brant Western," Jo chided him from her bed. "She's a lovely young woman, not some…some pin-up poster off your Internet."

When they were randy teenagers, Jo had frequently lectured them not to objectify women. Brant must have remembered the familiar refrain as well, Quinn thought, as the deep dimples Quinn despised flashed for just a moment with his smile.

"Sorry, Jo. But she was always the prettiest girl at PG High. I used to get tongue-tied if she only walked past me in the hall."

She was still the prettiest thing Quinn had seen in a long time. And he didn't even want to think about how delectable she tasted or the sexy little sounds she made when his mouth covered hers.…

Easton walked in, jarring him from yet another damn flashback.

"I reached Tess on her cell phone. She's off today but she's going to come over anyway. And I talked to Jake Dalton and he's stopping by on his way up to Cold Creek."

Pine Gulch's doctor had been raised on a huge cattle ranch at the head of Cold Creek Canyon, Quinn knew.

"Shouldn't we take her to the hospital or something?" Brant asked.

Quinn and Easton exchanged glances since they had frequently brought up the subject, but Jo spoke before he could answer.

"No hospital." Jo's voice was firm, stronger than he had heard it since he arrived. "I'm done with them. I'm dying and no doctor or hospital can change that. I want to go right here, in the house I shared with Guff, surrounded by those I love."

Brant blinked at her bluntness and Quinn sympathized with him. It was one thing to understand intellectually that her condition was terminal. It was quite another to hear her speak in such stark, uncompromising terms about it. He at least had had a few days to get used to the hard reality.

"But it's not going to happen today or even tomorrow," she went on. "I won't let it. Not until Cisco comes home. I just need to rest for a while and then I want to have a good long talk with you about what you've been doing for the army."

Brant released a heavy breath, his tired features still looking as if he had just been run over by a Humvee.

Quinn could completely sympathize with him. He could only hope Jo held out long enough so his people could track down the last of the Four Winds.

Chapter Nine

"What's the verdict?" Jo asked. "Is my heart still beating?"

Tess pulled the stethoscope away from Jo's brachial artery and pulled the blood pressure cuff off with a loud ripping sound.

She related Jo's blood pressure aloud to Jake Dalton, who frowned at the low diastolic and systolic numbers.

"Let's take a listen to your ticker," Pine Gulch's only doctor said, pulling out his own stethoscope.

Jo responded by glaring at Tess. "Dirty trick, bringing Jake along with you."

"I told you I called him," Easton said from the doorway of the room, where she stood with Quinn and the very solemn-looking Major Western. Tess purposely avoided looking at any of them, especially Quinn.

It was a darn good thing Jake wasn't checking her heart rate right about now. She had a feeling it would be galloping along faster than one of the Winder Ranch horses in an open pasture on a sunny afternoon.

Knowing Quinn was only a few feet away watching her out of those silver-blue eyes was enough to tangle her insides and make her palms itch with nerves.

"And I told you I don't need a doctor," Jo replied.

"Be careful or you'll hurt my feelings," Jake teased.

"Oh, poof. Your skin is thicker than rawhide."

"Yet you can still manage to break my heart again and again."

Jo laughed and Tess smiled along with her. Jake Dalton was one of her favorite people. He had been a rock to her after she moved back to Pine Gulch with Scott. Though her husband had a vast team of specialists in Idaho Falls, Jake had always been her first line of defense whenever she needed a medical opinion about something.

He was a good, old-fashioned small-town doctor, willing to make house calls and take worried phone calls at all hours of the day and night and treat all his patients like family.

She had been thrilled four years earlier when he married Maggie Cruz, a nurse practitioner who often volunteered with hospice. She now considered both of them among her dearest friends.

"This is all a lot of nonsense for nothing," Jo insisted. "I was a little overexcited when Brant arrived, that's all."

Jake said nothing, only examined her chart carefully. He asked Jo several questions about her pain level and whether she had passed out any other times she had neglected to tell them all about.

When he was finished, he smoothed a gentle hand over her hair. "I'm going to make a few changes in your meds. Why don't you get some rest and I'll explain what I want to do with Tess, okay?"

Tess knew it was an indication of Jo's weakened condition that she didn't argue, only nodded and closed her eyes.

Jake led the way out into the hall where the others waited. He closed the door behind him and headed for the kitchen, which Tess had learned long ago was really Command Central of Winder Ranch.

"What's happening?" Easton was the first to speak.

Jake's mouth tightened and his eyes looked bleak. "Her organs are starting to shut down. I'm sorry."

Even though Tess had been expecting it for days now, she was still saddened by the stark diagnosis.

"Which means what?" Brant asked. He looked very much the quintessential soldier with his close-cropped brown hair, strong jaw and sheer physical presence.

"It won't be long now," Jake said. "A couple of days, maybe."

Easton let out a long breath that wasn't quite a sob but probably would have been if she had allowed it.

Tess reached out and gripped her hand and Easton clutched her fingers tightly.

"I think it's time to think about round-the-clock nursing," Jake said. "I'm thinking more of her comfort and, to be honest, yours as well."

"Of course," Quinn said. "Absolutely. Whatever she needs."

Tess's chest ached at his unhesitating devotion to Jo.

Dr. Dalton nodded his approval. "I'll talk to hospice and see what they can provide."

Tess knew what the answer would be. Hospice was overburdened right now. She knew the agency didn't have the resources for that level of care.

"I'll do it. If you'll let me."

"You?" Brant asked, and she gave an inward flinch at the shock in his voice. Here was yet another person who only saw her as the silly girl she had been and she wondered if she would ever be able to escape her past.

"Right now the agency is understaffed," she answered. "I know they don't have the resources to have someone here all the time, as much as they would like to. They're going to recommend hospitalization in Idaho Falls for her last few days."

"She so wants to be here." Easton's voice trembled on the words.

"Barring that, they're going to tell you you'll have to hire a private nurse. I'd like to be that private nurse. I won't let you pay me but I want to do this for Jo. I'll make arrangements for the others to cover all my shifts and stay here, if that's acceptable to you all."

Tess refused to look at Quinn as she made the offer, though she could feel the heat of his gaze on her.

Part of her wondered at the insanity of offering to put herself in even closer proximity with him, but she knew he would be far too preoccupied to spend an instant thinking about a few regrettable moments of shared passion.

"I think it's a wonderful idea, if you're sure you're

up to it," Brant said, surprising her. "Quinn and Easton both tell me you're the best of her nurses."

"Are you sure?" Easton asked with a searching look.

"Absolutely. Let me do this for her and for you," she said to her friend.

"What do you think?" Easton turned to Quinn, and Tess finally risked a glance in his direction. She found him watching the scene with an unreadable expression in his silver-blue eyes.

"It seems a good solution if Tess is willing. Better than bringing in some stranger. But we *will* pay you."

She didn't argue with him, though she determined she would donate anything the family insisted on back to hospice, which had been one of Jo's favorite charities even before she had need of their services.

"I'll need a little time to make all the arrangements but I should be back in a few hours," she said.

"Thank you." Easton squeezed her fingers. "I don't know how we'll ever repay you."

"I'll see you in a few hours."

She said goodbye to Dr. Dalton and headed for the door. To her shock, Quinn followed her.

"I'll walk you out," he said gruffly, and her mind instantly filled with images from the last time he had walked her outside, when they had given into the intimacy of the night and the heat simmering between them.

She wanted to tell him she didn't need any more of his escorts, thanks very much, but she didn't want to remind him of those few moments.

"Why?" Quinn asked when they were outside.

She didn't need to ask what he meant. "I love her," she said simply.

His gaze narrowed and she could tell he wasn't convinced.

"Have you done this before? Round-the-clock nursing?"

She arched an eyebrow. "You mean besides the six years I cared for my husband?"

"I keep forgetting that."

She sighed, knowing he was only concerned for his foster mother. "I won't lie to you, it's always difficult at the end. The work is demanding and the emotional toll can be great. But if I can bring Jo a little bit of comfort and peace, I don't care about that."

"I don't get you," he muttered.

"I'm not that complicated."

He made a rough sound of disbelief low in his throat. He looked as if he wanted to say more but he finally just shook his head and opened the car door for her.

Two hours later, Tess set her small suitcase down in the guest room on the first floor, right next door to Jo's sickroom.

"This should work out fine," she said to Easton. It was a lovely room, one she hadn't seen before, filled with antiques and decorated in sage and pale peach.

She found it restful and calm and inherently feminine, with the lacy counterpane on the bed and the scrollwork on the bed frame and the light pine dresser.

Where did the others sleep? she wondered. Her insides trembled a little at the thought of Quinn somewhere in the house.

Why did sharing a house with him feel so different,

so much more intimate, than all those other days when she had come in and out at various hours to care for Jo?

"I hope I'm not kicking someone else out of a bed."

"Not at all." Easton smiled, though she wore the shadow of her grief like a black lace veil. "No worries. We've got room to spare. There are plenty of beds in this place, plus the bunkhouse and the foreman's house, which are empty right now since my foreman has his own place down the canyon."

"That's where you were raised, wasn't it? The foreman's house?"

Easton nodded. "Until I was sixteen, when my parents were killed in a car accident and I moved here with Aunt Jo and Uncle Guff. The boys were all gone by then and it was only me."

"You must have missed them."

Easton smiled as she settled on the bed, wrapping her arms around her knees. "The house always seemed too empty without them. I adored them and missed them like crazy. Even though I was so much younger—Quinn was five years older, Brant four and Cisco three—they were always kind to me. I still don't know why but they never seemed to mind me tagging along. Three instant older cousins who felt more like brothers was heady stuff for an only child like me."

"I was always jealous of my friends who had older brothers to look out for them," Tess said.

"I loved it. One time, Quinn found out an older boy at school was teasing me because I had braces and glasses. Roy Hargrove. Did you ever know him? He would have been a couple years younger than you."

"Oh, right. Greasy hair. Big hands."

Easton laughed. "That's the one. He used to call me some terrible names and one day Quinn found me crying about it. To this day, I have no idea what the boys said to him. But not only did Roy stop calling me names, he went out of his way to completely avoid me and always got this scared look in his eyes when he saw me, until his family moved away a few years later."

Easton smiled a little at the memory. "Anyway, there's plenty of room here at the house. Eight bedrooms, counting the two down here."

Tess stared at her friend. "Eight? I've never been upstairs but I had no idea the house was that big!"

"Guff and Jo wanted to fill them all with children but it wasn't to be. Jo was almost forty when they met and married and she'd already had cancer once and had to have a hysterectomy because of it. I think they thought about adopting but they ended up opening the ranch to foster children instead, especially after Quinn came. His mother and Jo were cousins, did you know that? So we're cousins by marriage, somehow."

"I had no idea," she exclaimed.

"Jo and his mother were good friends when they were younger but then they lost track of each other. From what I understand, it took Jo a long time to get custody of him after his parents died."

"How old were you when they moved here?"

"I was almost ten when Quinn came. He would have been fourteen."

Tess remembered him, all rough-edged and full of attitude. He had been dark and gorgeous and dangerous, even back then.

"Brant moved in after Quinn had been here about four months, but you probably already knew him from school."

She knew Brant used to live on a small ranch in the canyon with his family. He had been in her grade and Tess always remembered him as wearing rather raggedy clothes and a few times he had come to school with an arm in a sling or bruises on his arms. Just like Quinn, Brant Western hadn't been like the other boys, either. He had been solemn and quiet, smart but not pushy about it.

She had been so self-absorbed as a girl that she hadn't known until years later that the Winders had taken Brant away from his abusive home life, though she had noticed around middle school that he started dressing better and seemed more relaxed.

"And then Cisco moved in a few months after Brant." Easton spoke the words briskly and rose from the bed, but not before Tess caught a certain something in her eyes. Tess had noticed it before whenever Easton mentioned the other man's name but she sensed Easton didn't want to discuss it.

"Jo and Guff had other foster children over the years, didn't they?"

"A few here and there but usually only as a temporary stopping point." She shrugged. "I think they would have had more but…after my parents died, I was pretty shattered for a while and I think they were concerned about subdividing their attention among others when I was grieving and needed them."

Her heart squeezed with sympathy for Easton's loss. She couldn't imagine losing both parents at the same time. Her father's death a few years after Scott's accident had been tough enough. She didn't know how she would have survived if her mother had died, too.

"They have always been there for me," Easton said quietly.

Tess instinctively reached out and hugged her friend. Easton returned the embrace for only a moment before she stepped away.

"Thank you again for agreeing to stay." Her voice wobbled only a little. "Let me know if you need anything."

"I will. Right back at you. Even just a shoulder to cry on. I might be here as Jo's nurse but I'm your friend, too."

Easton pulled open the door. "I know. That's why I love you. You're just the kind of person I want to be when I grow up, Tess."

Her laugh was abrupt. "You need to set your sights a little higher than me. Now Jo, that's another story. There's something for both of us to shoot for."

"I think if I tried the rest of my life, I wouldn't be able to measure up to her. She's an original."

Chapter Ten

The entire ranch seemed to be holding its collective breath.

Day-to-day life at the ranch went on as usual. The stock needed to be watered, the human inhabitants needed food and sleep, laundry still piled up.

But everyone was mechanically going through the motions, caught up in the larger human drama taking place in this room.

Forty-eight hours later, Tess sat by the window in Jo's sickroom, her hands busy with the knitting needles she had learned to wield during the long years of caring for Scott. She had made countless baby blankets and afghans during those years, donating most of them to the hospital in Idaho Falls or to the regional pediatric center in Salt Lake City.

Jo coughed, raspy and dry, and Tess set the unfinished blanket aside and rose to lift the water bottle from the side of the bed and hold the straw to Jo's mouth.

Her patient sipped a little, then turned her head away.

"Thank you," she murmured.

"What else can I get you?" Tess asked.

"Cisco. Only Cisco."

Her heart ached for Jo. The woman was in severe pain, her organs failing, but she clung to life, determined to see her other foster son one more time. Tess wanted desperately to give her that final gift so she could at last say goodbye.

A few moments later, Jo rested back against the pillow and closed her eyes. She didn't open them when Easton pushed open the door.

Tess pressed a finger to her mouth and moved out into the hall.

"I came to relieve you for a few moments. Why don't you go outside and stretch your legs for a while? Go get some fresh air."

She nodded, grateful Easton could spell her for a few moments, though she had no intention of going outside yet. "Thanks. I'll be back in a few moments."

"Take your time. I'm done with the morning chores and have a couple hours."

When Easton closed Jo's door behind her, Tess turned toward the foyer. Instead of going outside, though, she headed up the stairs toward the empty bedroom Quinn had taken over for an office while he was in Pine Gulch.

She approached the open doorway, mortified that her heart was pounding from more than just the fast climb up the stairs.

She heard Quinn's raised voice before she reached the doorway, sounding more heated than she had heard him since that long-ago day she had accused him of cheating.

He sat with his back to the door at a long writing desk near the window. From the angle of the doorway, she could see a laptop in front of him with files strewn across the surface of the desk.

He wore a soft gray shirt with the sleeves rolled up and she could see his strong, muscled forearm flex. His dark hair looked a little tousled, as if he had run his fingers through it recently, which she had learned was his habit.

She wasn't sure which version of the man she found more appealing. The rugged cowboy who had ridden to Windy Lake, his hands sure and confident on the reins and his black Stetson pulled low over his face. The loving, devoted son who sat beside Jo's bedside for long hours, reading to her from the newspaper or the Bible or whatever Jo asked of him.

Or this one, driven and committed, forcing himself to put aside the crisis in his personal life to focus on business and the employees and customers who depended on him.

She gave an inaudible sigh. The truth was, she was drawn to every facet of the dratted man and was more fascinated by him with every passing hour.

Jo. She was here for Jo, she reminded herself.

"Look, whatever it takes," he said into the phone. "I'm tired of this garbage. Find him! I don't care what you have to do!"

After pressing a button on the phone, he threw it onto the desk with such force that she couldn't contain a little gasp.

He turned at the sound and something flared in his

eyes, something raw and intense, before he quickly banked it. "What is it? Is she..."

"No. Nothing like that. Was that phone call about Cisco?"

"Supposed to be. But as you can probably tell, I'm hitting walls everywhere I turn. That was the consulate in El Salvador. He was there a few weeks ago but nobody knows where he is now. I have tried every contact I have and I can't manage to find one expatriate American in Latin America."

She walked into the room, picking her words carefully. "I don't think she's going to be able to hang on until he gets here, though she's trying her best."

"I hate that I can't give her this."

"It's not your fault, Quinn." She curled her fingers to her palm in an effort to fight the impulse to touch his arm in comfort, as she would have done to Easton and even Brant, who, except for those first few moments when he arrived, had treated her with nothing but kindness and respect.

Quinn was different. Somehow she couldn't relax in his company, not with their shared past and the more recent heat that unfurled inside her whenever he was near.

She let out a breath, wishing she could regard him the same as she did everyone else.

"Sometimes you have to accept you've tried your best," she said.

"Have I?" The frustration in his voice reached something deep inside her and this time she couldn't resist the urge to touch his arm.

"What else can you do? You can't go after him."

He looked down at her pale fingers against the

darker skin of his arm for a long moment. When he lifted his gaze, she swallowed at the sudden intensity in his silver-blue gaze.

She pulled her hand away and tucked it into the pocket of her scrubs. "When you've done all you can, sometimes you have no choice but to put your problems in God's hands."

His expression turned hard, cynical. "A lovely sentiment. Did that help you sleep at night when you were caring for your husband?"

She drew in a sharp breath then let it out quickly, reminding herself he was responding from a place of pain she was entirely familiar with.

"As a matter of fact, it did," she answered evenly.

"Sorry." He raked a hand through his hair again, messing it further. "That was unnecessarily harsh."

"You want to fix everything. That's understandable. It's what you do, isn't it?"

"Not this time. I can't fix this."

The bleakness in his voice tore at her heart and she couldn't help herself, she rested her fingers on his warm arm again. "I'm sorry. I know how terribly hard this is for you."

He looked anguished and before she quite realized what he was doing, he pulled her into his arms and clung tightly to her. He didn't kiss her, only held her. She froze in shock for just a moment then she wrapped her arms around him and let him draw whatever small comfort she could offer from the physical connection with another person. Sometimes a single quiet embrace could offer more comfort than a hundred condolences, she knew.

They stood for several moments in silence with his

arms around her, his breath a whisper against her hair. Something sweet and intangible—and even tender— passed between them. She was afraid to move or even breathe for fear of ruining this moment, this chance to provide him a small measure of peace.

All too soon, he exhaled a long breath and dropped his arms, moving away a little, and she felt curiously bereft.

He looked astonished and more than a little embarrassed.

"I... Sorry. I don't know what that was about. Sorry."

She smiled gently. "You're doing your best," she repeated. "Jo understands that."

He opened his mouth to answer but before he could, Brant's voice sounded from downstairs, loud and irate.

"It's about damn time you showed up."

Tess blinked. In her limited experience, the officer was invariably patient with everyone, a sea of calm in the emotional tumult of Winder Ranch. She had never heard that sort of harshness from him.

In response, she heard another man's voice, one she didn't recognize.

"I'm not too late, am I?"

Quinn's expression reflected her own shock as both of them realized Francisco Del Norte had at last arrived.

Quinn took the stairs two at a time. She followed with the same urgency, a little concerned the men might come to blows—at least judging by Brant's anger and that hot expression in Quinn's eyes as he had rushed past her.

In the foyer, she found Brant and Quinn facing off against a hard-eyed, rough-looking Latino who bore little resemblance to the laughing, mischievous boy she remembered from school.

"Where the hell have you been?" Quinn snapped.

Fatigue clouded the other man's dark eyes. Tess wasn't sure she had ever seen anyone look so completely exhausted.

"Long story. I could tell you, but you know the drill. Then I'd have to kill you and I'm too damn tired right now to take on both your sorry asses at the same time."

The three men eyed each other for another moment and Tess held her breath, wondering if she ought to step in. Then, as if by some unspoken signal, they all moved together and gave that shoulder-slap thing men did instead of hugging.

"Tell me I'm not too late." Cisco's voice was taut with anguish.

"Not yet. But she's barely hanging on, man. She was just waiting to say goodbye to you."

Tears filled Cisco's eyes as he uttered a quick prayer of gratitude in Spanish.

She was inclined to dislike the man for the worry he had put everyone through these past few days and for Jo's heartache. But she couldn't help feeling compassion for the undisguised sorrow in his eyes.

"They didn't… I didn't get the message until three days ago. I was in the middle of something big and it took me a while to squeeze my way out."

Brant and Quinn didn't look appeased by the explanation but they didn't seem inclined to push him either.

"Can I see her?"

Both Brant and Quinn turned to look at Tess, still standing on the stairs, as if she was Jo's guardian and gatekeeper.

"Easton's in with her. I'll go see if she's awake."

She turned away, but not before she caught an odd expression flicker across his features at the mention of Easton's name.

She left the three men and walked down the hall to Jo's bedroom. When she carefully eased open the door, emotions clogged her throat at the scene she found inside.

Easton was the one asleep now, with her head resting on the bed beside her aunt. Jo's frail, gnarled hand rested on her niece's hair.

Jo pressed a finger to her mouth. Though she tried to shake her head, she was so weak she barely moved against the pillow.

"It's not time for more meds, is it?" she murmured, her voice thready.

Though Tess could barely hear the woman's whisper, Easton still opened her eyes and jerked her head up.

"Sorry. I must have just dozed off."

Jo smiled. "Just a few minutes ago, dear. Not long enough."

"It's not time for meds," Tess answered her. "I was only checking to see if you were awake and up for a visitor."

Though she thought she spoke calmly enough, some clue in her demeanor must have alerted them something had happened. Both women looked at her carefully.

"What is it?" Easton asked.

Before she could answer, she heard a noise in the doorway and knew without turning around that Cisco had followed her.

Easton's features paled and she scrambled to her feet. Tess registered her reaction for only an instant, then she was completely disarmed when the hard, dangerous-looking man hurried to Jo's bedside, his eyes still wet with emotion.

The joy in Jo's features was breathtakingly beautiful as she reached a hand to caress his cheek. "You're here. Oh, my dear boy, you're here at last."

Quinn and Brant followed Cisco into the room. Tess watched their reunion for a moment, then she quietly slipped from the room to give them the time and space they needed together.

Chapter Eleven

The woman Quinn loved as a mother took her last breath twelve hours after Cisco Del Norte returned to Winder Ranch.

With all four of them around her bedside and Tess standing watchfully on the edge of the room, Jo succumbed to the ravages cancer had wrought on her frail body.

Quinn had had plenty of time to prepare. He had known weeks ago her condition was terminal and he had been at the ranch for nearly ten days to spend these last days with her and watch her inexorable decline.

He had known it was coming. That didn't make it any easier to watch her draw one ragged breath into her lungs, let it out with a sigh and then nothing more.

Beside him, Easton exhaled a soft, choked sob. He

wrapped an arm around her shoulder and pulled her close, aware that Cisco, on her other side, had made the same move but had checked it when Quinn reached her first.

"I'll call Dr. Dalton and let him know," Tess murmured after a few moments of leaving them to their shared sorrow.

He met her gaze, deeply grateful for her quiet calm. "Thank you."

She held his gaze for a moment, her own filled with an echo of his grief, then she smiled. "You're welcome."

He had fully expected the loss, this vast chasm of pain. But he hadn't anticipated the odd sense of peace that seemed to have settled over all of them to know Jo's suffering was finally over.

A big part of that was due to Tess and her steady, unexpected strength, he admitted over the next hour as they worked with the doctor and the funeral home to make arrangements.

She seemed to know exactly what to say, what to do, and he was grateful to turn these final responsibilities over to her.

If he found comfort in anything right now, it was in the knowledge that Jo had spent her last days surrounded by those she loved and by the tender care Tess had provided.

He couldn't help remembering that embrace with Tess upstairs in his office. Those few moments with her arms around him and her cheek resting against his chest had been the most peaceful he had known since he arrived at the ranch.

He had found them profoundly moving, for reasons he couldn't explain, anymore than he could explain how the person he thought he despised most in the world ended up being the one he turned to in his greatest need.

He was lousy at doing nothing.

The evening after Jo's funeral, Quinn sat at the kitchen table at the ranch with a heaping plate of leftovers in front of him and an aching restlessness twisting through him.

The past three days since Jo's death had been a blur of condolence visits from neighbors, of making plans with Southerland Shipping for the corporate jet to return for him by the end of the week, of seeing to the few details Jo hadn't covered in the very specific funeral arrangements she made before her death.

Most of those details fell on his shoulders by default, simply because nobody else was around much.

He might have expected them to all come together in their shared grief but each of Jo's Four Winds seemed to be dealing with her death in a unique way.

Easton took refuge out on the ranch, with her horses and her cattle and hard, punishing work. Brant had left the night Jo died for his own ranch, a mile or so up the canyon and had only been back a few times and for the funeral earlier. Cisco slept for a full thirty-six hours as if it had been months since he closed his eyes. As soon as the funeral was over earlier that day, he had taken one of the ranch horses and a bedroll and said he needed to sleep under the stars.

As for Quinn, he focused on what work he could do long-distance and on these last few details for Jo. Staying busy helped push the pain away a little.

He sipped at his beer as the old house creaked and settled around him and the furnace kicked in with a low whoosh against the late October cold. Forlorn sounds, he thought. Lonely, even.

Maybe Cisco had the right idea. Maybe he ought to just get the hell out of Dodge, grab one of the horses and ride hard and fast into the mountains.

The thought did have a certain appeal.

Or maybe he ought to just call his pilot and move up his departure. He could be home by midnight.

What would be the difference between sitting alone at his house in Seattle or sitting alone here at Winder Ranch? This aching emptiness would follow him every-where for a while, he was afraid, until that inevitable day when the loss would begin to fade a little.

Hovering on the edge of his mind was the awareness that once he left Winder Ranch this time, he would have very few reasons to return. With Jo and Guff gone, his anchor to the place had been lifted.

Easton would always be here. He could still come back to visit her, but with Brant in the military and Cisco off doing whatever mysterious things occupied his time, nothing would ever be the same.

The Four Winds would be scattered once more.

Jo had been their true north, their center. Without her, a chapter in his life was ending and the realization left him more than a little bereft.

He rose suddenly as that restlessness sharpened, in-tensified. He couldn't just sit here. He didn't really feel like spending the night on the hard ground, but at least he could take one of the horses out for a hard moonlit ride to work off some of this energy.

The thought inevitably touched off memories of the other ride he had taken into the mountains just days ago—and of the woman he had been doing his best not to think about for the past few days.

Tess had packed up all the medical equipment in Jo's room and had left the ranch the night Jo died. He had seen her briefly at the funeral, a slim, lovely presence in a bright yellow dress amid all the traditionally dark mourning clothes. Jo would have approved, he remembered thinking. She would have wanted bright colors and light and sunshine at her funeral. He only wished he'd been the one to think of it and had put on a vibrant tie instead of the muted, conservative one he had worn with his suit.

To his regret, Tess had slipped away from the service before he had a chance to talk to her. Now he found himself remembering again those stunning few moments they had shared upstairs in his office bedroom, when she had simply held him, offering whatever solace he could draw from her calm embrace.

He missed her.

Quinn let out a breath. Several times over the past days, as he dealt with details, he had found himself wanting to turn to her for her unique perspective on something, for some of her no-nonsense advice, or just to see her smile at some absurdity.

Ridiculous. How had she become so important to him in just a matter of days? It was only the stress of the circumstances, he assured himself.

But right now as he stood in the Winder Ranch kitchen with this emptiness yawning inside him, he had a desperate ache to see her again.

She would know just the right thing to say to ease his spirit. Somehow he knew it.

If he just showed up on her doorstep for no reason, she would probably think he was an idiot. He couldn't say he only wanted her to hold him again, to ease the restlessness of his spirit.

His gaze fell on a hook by the door and fate smiled on him when he recognized her jacket hanging next to his own denim ranch coat. He had noticed it the day before and remembered her wearing it a few nights when she had come to the ranch, before she moved into the spare room, but he had forgotten about it until just this moment.

If he gave it a moment's thought, he knew he would talk himself out of seeing her while his heart was still raw and aching.

So he decided not to think about it.

He shrugged into his own jacket, then grabbed hers off the hook by the door and headed into the night.

The nature of hospice work meant she had to face death on a fairly consistent basis but it never grew any easier—and some losses hit much harder than others.

Tess had learned early, though, that it was best to throw herself into a project, preferably something physical and demanding, while the pain was still raw and fresh. When she could exhaust her body as much as her spirit, she had half a chance of sleeping at night without dreams, tangled-up nightmares of all those she had loved and lost.

The evening of Jo's funeral, she stood on a stepladder in the room that once had been Scott's, scraping layers of paint off the wide wooden molding that encircled the high ceiling of the room.

Stripping the trim in this room down and refinishing the natural wood had always been in her plans when she bought the house after Scott's accident but she had never gotten around to it, too busy with his day-to-day care.

She supposed it was ironic that she was only getting around to doing the work she wanted on the room now that the house was for sale. She ought to leave the re-decorating for the new owners to apply their own tastes, but it seemed the perfect project to keep her mind and body occupied as best she could.

The muscles of her arms ached from reaching above her head but that didn't stop her from scraping in rhythm to the loud honky-tonk music coming from her iPod dock in the corner of the empty room.

She was singing along about a two-timin' man so loudly she nearly missed the low musical chime of her doorbell over the wails.

Though she wasn't at all in the mood to talk to anyone, she used any excuse to drop her arms to give her aching muscles a rest.

She thought about ignoring the doorbell, certain it must be her mother dropping by to check on her. She knew Maura was concerned that Jo's death would hit her hard and she wasn't sure she was in the mood to deal with her maternal worry.

Her mother would have seen the lights and her car in the driveway and Tess knew she would just keep stubbornly ringing the bell until her daughter answered.

She sighed and stepped down from the ladder.

"Coming," she called out. "Hang on."

She took a second before she pulled open the door to tuck in a stray curl slipping from the folded bandanna that held her unruly hair away from her face while she worked.

"Sorry, I was up on the ladder and it took me a minute…"

Her voice trailed off and she stared in shock. That definitely wasn't her mother standing on her small porch. Her heart picked up a beat.

"Quinn! Hello."

"Hi. May I come in?" he prompted, when she continued to stare at him, baffled as to why he might be standing on her doorstep.

"Oh. Of course."

She stepped back to allow him inside, fervently wishing she was wearing something a little more presentable than her scruffiest pair of jeans and the disreputable faded cropped T-shirt she used for gardening.

"Were you expecting someone else?"

"I thought you might be my mother. She still lives in town, though my father died a few years back. He had a heart attack on the golf course. Shocked us all. Friends have tried to talk my mother into moving somewhere warmer but she claims she likes it here. I think she's really been sticking around to keep an eye on me. Maybe she'll finally move south when I take off for Portland."

She clamped her mouth shut when she realized she was babbling, something she rarely did. She also registered the rowdy music coming from down the hall.

"Sorry. Let me grab that music."

She hurried back to the bedroom and turned off the iPod, then returned to her living room, where she saw him looking at the picture frames clustered across the top of her upright piano.

He looked gorgeous, she thought, in a Stetson and a denim jacket that made him look masculine and rough.

Her insides did a long, slow roll but she quickly pushed back her reaction, especially when she saw the slightly lost expression in his eyes.

"I'm sorry," she said. "I was stripping paint off the wall trim in my spare bedroom. I...needed the distraction. What can I do for you?"

He held out his arm, along with something folded and blue. "You left your coat at the ranch. I thought you might need it."

She took it from him and didn't miss the tiny flicker of static that jumped from his skin to hers. Something just as electric sparked in his eyes at the touch.

"You didn't need to drive all the way into town to return it. I could have picked it up from Easton some other time."

He shrugged. "I guess you're not the only one who needed a distraction. Everybody else took off tonight in different directions and I just didn't feel like hanging around the ranch by myself."

He didn't look at her when he spoke, but she recognized the edgy restlessness in his silver-blue eyes. She wanted to reach out to him, as she might have done with anyone else, but she didn't trust herself around him and she didn't know if he would welcome her touch. Though he had that day at the ranch, she remembered.

"How are you at scraping paint?" she asked on impulse, then wanted to yank the words back when she realized the absurdity of putting him to work in her spare room just hours after his foster mother's funeral.

He didn't look upset by the question. "I've scraped the Winder Ranch barn and outbuildings in my day but never done room trim. Is this any different?"

"Harder," she said frankly. "This house has been

through ten owners in its seventy-five years of existence and I swear every single one of them except me
has left three or four layers of paint. It's sweaty, hard,
frustrating work."

"In that case, bring it on."

She laughed and shook her head. "You don't know
what you're getting into, but if you're sure you're
willing to help, I would welcome the company."

It wasn't a lie, she thought as she led him back to the
bedroom after he left his jacket and hat on the living-
room couch. She had to admit she was grateful to have
someone to talk to and for one last opportunity to see
him again before he left Pine Gulch.

"You don't really have to do this," she said when they
reached the room. "You're welcome to stay, even if you
don't want to work."

Odd how what she had always considered a good-
size space seemed to shrink in an instant. She could
smell him, sexy and masculine, and she wished again
that she wasn't dressed in work clothes.

"Where can I start?"

"I was up on the ladder working on the ceiling trim.
If you would like to start around the windows, that
would be great."

"Deal."

He rolled up the sleeves of his shirt that looked expensive and tailored—not that she knew much about
men's clothes—and grabbed a paint scraper. Without
another word, he set immediately to work.

Tess watched him for a moment, then turned the
music on again, switching to a little more mellow music.

For a long time, they worked without speaking. She

didn't find the silence awkward in the slightest, merely contemplative on both their parts.

Quinn seemed just as content not to make aimless conversation and though she was intensely aware of him on the other side of the room, she wasn't sure he even remembered she was in the room until eight or nine songs into the playlist.

"My father killed my mother when I was thirteen years old."

He said the abrupt words almost dispassionately but she heard the echo of a deep, vast pain in his voice.

She set down her scraper, her heart aching for him even as she held her breath that he felt he could share something so painful with her now, out of the blue like this.

"Oh, Quinn. I'm so sorry."

He released a long, slow breath, like air escaping from a leaky valve, and she wondered how long he had kept the memories bottled deep inside him.

"It happened twenty years ago but every moment of that night is as clear in my mind as the ride we took to Windy Lake last week. Clearer, even."

She climbed down the ladder. "You were there?"

He continued moving the scraper across the wood and tiny multicolored flakes of paint fluttered to the floor. "I was there. But I couldn't stop it."

She leaned against the wall beside him, hesitant to say the wrong word that might make him regret sharing this part of his past with her.

"What happened?" she murmured, sensing he needed to share it. Perhaps this was all part of his grieving process for Jo, the woman who had taken him in and helped him heal from his ugly, painful past.

"They were fighting, as usual. My parents' marriage was…difficult. My father was an attorney who worked long hours. When he returned home, he always insisted on a three-course dinner on the table, no matter what hour of the day or night, and he wanted the house completely spotless."

"That must have been hard for a young boy."

"I guess I was lucky. He didn't take his bad moods out on me. Only on her."

She held her breath, waiting for the rest.

"Their fighting woke me up," Quinn said after a moment, "and I heard my dad start to get a little rough. Also usual. I went down to stop it. That didn't always work but sometimes a little diversion did the trick. Not this time."

He scraped harder and she wanted to urge him to spare himself the anguish of retelling the story, but again, she had that odd sense that he needed to share this, for reasons she didn't understand.

"My dad was in a rage, accusing her of sleeping with one of the other attorneys in his firm."

"Was she?"

He shrugged. "I don't know. Maybe. My father was a bastard but she seemed to delight in finding and hitting every one of his hot buttons. She laughed at him. I'll never forget the sound of her laughing, with her face still bruised and red where he had slapped her. She said she was having a torrid affair with the other man, that he was much better in bed than my father."

She drew in a sharp breath, hating the thought of a thirteen-year-old version of Quinn witnessing such ugliness between his parents.

"I don't know," he went on. "She might have been lying. Theirs was not a healthy relationship, in any sense of the word. He needed to be in control of everything and she needed to be constantly adored."

She thought of Quinn being caught in the middle of it all and her chest ached for him and she had to curl her fingers into her palms to keep from reaching for him.

"My father said he wasn't going to let her make a fool out of him any longer. He walked out of the room and I thought for sure he was going to pack a suitcase and leave. I was happy, you know. For those few moments, I was thinking how much better things would be without him. No more yelling, no more fights."

"But he didn't leave."

He gave a rough laugh and set the scraper down and sat beside her on the floor, his back against the wall and their elbows touching. "He didn't leave. He came out of the bedroom with the .38 he kept locked in a box by the side of his bed. He shot her three times. Twice in the heart and then once more in the head. And then he turned the gun on himself."

"Oh, dear God."

"I couldn't stop it. For a long time, I kept asking myself if I could have done something. Said something. I just stood there."

She couldn't help herself, she covered his hand with hers. After a long moment, he turned his hand and twisted his fingers with hers, holding tight. They sat that way, shoulders brushing while the music on her playlist shifted to a slow, jazzy ballad.

She kept envisioning that rough-edged, angry boy he had been when he first came to Pine Gulch. He must have been consumed with pain and guilt over his parents' murder-suicide. She could see it so clearly, just as she saw in grim detail her own awful behavior toward him, simply because he had refused to pay any attention to her.

"I am so, so sorry, Quinn," she murmured, for everything he had survived and for her own part in making life harder for him here.

"The first year after was…hellish," he said, his voice low. "That's the only word that fits. I was thrown into the foster-care system and spent several months bouncing from placement to placement."

"None of them stuck?"

"I wasn't an easy kid to love," he said. "You knew me when I first came to Pine Gulch. I was angry and hurting and hated the world. Jo and Guff saw past all that. They saw whatever tiny spark of good might still be buried deep inside me and didn't stop until they helped me see it, too."

"I'm so happy you found each other."

"Same here." He paused, looking a little baffled. "I don't know why I'm telling you this. I didn't come here to dump it all on you. The truth is, I don't talk about it much. I don't think I've ever shared it with anybody but Brant and Cisco and Easton."

"It's natural to think about the circumstances that brought you into Jo's world. I imagine it's all connected for you."

"I was on a path to nowhere when Jo finally found me up in Boise and petitioned for custody. I was only the kid of a cousin. I'd never even met her but she and Guff still took me on, with all that baggage. She was a hell of a woman."

"I'm going to miss her dearly," Tess said quietly.

"But I keep trying to focus on how much better a person I am because I knew her."

Their hands were still entwined between them and she could feel the heat of his skin and the hard strength of his fingers.

"I don't know what to make of you," he finally said.

She gave a small laugh. "Why's that?"

"You baffle me. I don't know which version of you is real."

"All of it. I'm like every other woman. A mass of contradictions, most of which I don't even understand myself. Sometimes I'm a saint, sometimes I'm a bitch. Sometimes I'm the life of the party, sometimes I just want everybody to leave me alone. But mostly, I'm just a woman."

"That part I get."

The low timbre of his voice and the sudden light in his eyes sent a shower of sparks arcing through her. She was suddenly intensely aware of him—the breadth of his shoulder nudging hers, the glitter of silvery blue eyes watching her, the scent of him, of sage and bergamot and something else that was indefinable.

Her insides quivered and her pulse seemed to accelerate. "I don't regret many things in my life," she said, her voice breathy and low. "But I wish I could go back and change the way I treated you when we were younger. I hate that I gave you even a moment's unhappiness when you had already been through so much with your parents."

His shoulder shrugged beside her. "It was a long time ago, Tess. In the grand scheme of life, it didn't really mean anything."

"I was so awful to you."

"I wasn't exactly an easy person to like."

"That wasn't the problem. The opposite, actually. I…liked you too much," she confessed. "I hated that you thought I was some silly, brainless cheerleader. I wanted desperately for you to notice me."

His mouth quirked a little. "How could I help it?"

"You mean, when I was getting you kicked off the baseball team for cheating and then lying to my boyfriend and telling him you did something I only *wanted* you to do?"

"That's why Scott and his buddies beat me up that night? I had no idea."

"I'm so sorry, Quinn. I was despicable to you."

"Why?" he asked. "I still don't quite understand what I ever did to turn your wrath against me."

She sighed. "Every girl in school had a crush on you, but for me, it went way past crush. I didn't know your story but I could tell you were in pain. Maybe that's why you fascinated me, more than anyone I had ever known in my sheltered little life. I guess I was something of a healer, even then."

He gazed at her as the music shifted again, something low and sultry.

"I was fiercely attracted to you," she finally admitted. "But you made it clear you weren't interested. My pride was hurt. But I have to say, I think my heart was a little bruised, too. And so I turned mean. I wanted you to hurt, too. It was terrible and small of me and I'm so, so sorry."

"It was a long time ago," he said again. "We're both different people."

She smiled a little, her pulse pounding loudly in her ears. "Not so different," she murmured, still holding his hand. "I'm still fiercely attracted to you."

Chapter Twelve

Her breath snagged in her throat as she waited for him to break the sudden silence between them that seemed to drag on forever, though it was probably only several endless, excruciating seconds.

She braced herself, not sure she could survive another rejection. Nerves shivered through her as she waited for him to move, to speak, to do *anything.*

Just when she thought she couldn't endure the uncertainty another moment and was about to scramble away and tell him to ignore every single thing she had just said, he groaned her name and then his mouth captured hers in a wild kiss.

At that first stunning brush of his lips, the slick texture of his mouth, heat exploded between them like an August lightning storm on dry tinder. She returned his kiss, pouring everything into her response—her regret for the hurt she had caused him, her compassion for his loss, the soft tenderness blooming inside her.

And especially this urgent attraction pulsing to every corner of her body with each beat of her heart.

This was right. Inevitable, even. From the moment she heard him ring the doorbell earlier, some part of her had known they would end up here, with his arms around her and his heartbeat strong and steady under her fingers.

She wanted to help him, to heal him. To soak his pain inside her and ease his heart, if only for a moment.

She wrapped her arms more tightly around his neck, relishing the contrast between her curves and his immovable strength, between the cool wall at her back and all the glorious heat of his arms.

"While we're apologizing," he murmured against her mouth, "I'm sorry I was such an idiot the last time I kissed you. I don't have any excuse, other than fear."

She blinked at him, wondering why she had never noticed those dark blue speckles in his eyes. "Of what?"

"This. You." His mouth danced across hers again and everything feminine inside her sighed with delight.

"I want you." His voice was little more than a low rasp that sent every nerve ending firing madly. "I want you more than I've ever wanted another woman in my life and it scares the hell out of me."

"I'm just a woman. What's to be scared about?"

He laughed roughly. "That's like a saber-toothed tiger saying I'm just a nice little kitty. You are no ordinary woman, Tess."

Before she could figure out whether he meant the words as a compliment, he deepened the kiss and she decided she didn't care, as long as he continued this delicious assault on her senses.

He lowered her to the floor and she held him tightly as all the sleepy desires she had buried deep inside for years bubbled to the surface. It had been so long—so very, very long—since she had been held and cherished like this and she wanted to savor every second.

The taste of him, the scent of him, the implacable strength of his arms around her. It all felt perfect. *He* felt perfect.

She supposed that was silly, given the slightly unromantic circumstances. Instead of candlelight and rose petals and soft pillows, they were on the hard floor of her spare room with bright fluorescent lights gleaming.

But she wouldn't have changed any of it, especially at the risk of shattering this hazy, delicious cocoon of desire wrapped around them.

Okay, she might wish she were wearing something a little more sensual, especially when his hands went to the buttons of her old work shirt. But he didn't seem to mind her clothing, judging by the heavy-lidded hunger in his eyes after he had worked the buttons free and the plackets of her shirt fell away.

She should have felt exposed here in the unforgiving light of the room. Instead, she felt feminine and eminently desirable as his eyes darkened.

"You're gorgeous," he murmured. "The most beautiful thing I've ever seen."

"I'm afraid I'm not the tight-bodied cheerleader I was at sixteen."

"Who wants some silly cheerleader when he could have a saber-toothed tiger of a woman in his arms?"

She laughed but it turned into a ragged gasp when he slowly caressed her through the fabric of her bra, his fingers hard and masculine against her breast.

He groaned, low in his throat, and his thumb deftly traced the skin just above the lacy cup. Everything tightened inside her, a lovely swell of tension as he worked the clasp free, and she nearly arched off the floor when his fingers covered her skin.

He teased and explored her body while his mouth tantalized hers with deep, silky tastes and her hands explored the hard muscles of his back and the thick softness of his hair.

"This is crazy," he said after long, delirious moments. "It's not what I came here for, I swear."

"Don't think about it," she advised him, nipping little kisses down the warm column of his neck. "I know I'm not."

His laugh turned into a groan as she feathered more kisses along his jawline. "Well, when you put it that way…"

She smiled, then gasped when he began trailing kisses down the side of her throat. Every coherent thought skittered out of her head when his mouth found her breast. She tangled her hands in his hair, arching into his mouth as he tasted and teased.

Oh, heaven. She felt as if she had been waiting years just for this, just for him, as if everything inside her had been frozen away until he came back to Pine Gulch to thaw all those lonely, forgotten little corners of her heart.

She thought again how very perfect, inevitable, this was as he pulled her shirt off and then removed his own.

He was beautiful. The rough-edged, rebellious boy

had grown into a hard, dangerous man, all powerful muscles and masculine hollows and strength. She wanted to explore every single inch of that smooth skin.

She would, she vowed. Even if it took all night. Or several nights. It was a sacrifice she was fully willing to make.

Again she had that sense of inescapable destiny. They had been moving toward this moment since that first night he had startled her in the hallway of Winder Ranch. Longer, even. Maybe all that dancing around each other they had done in high school had just been a prelude to this.

A few moments later, no clothing barriers remained between them and she exulted in the sheer delicious wonder of his skin brushing hers, his strength surrounding her softness.

He kissed her and a restless need started deep inside her and expanded out in hot, hungry waves. She couldn't get enough of this, of him. She traced a hand over his pectoral muscles, feeling the leashed strength in him.

And then she forgot everything when he reached a hand between their bodies to the aching core of her hunger. She gasped his name, shifting restlessly against his fingers, and everything inside her coiled with a sweet, urgent ache of anticipation.

She felt edgy, panicky suddenly, as if the room were spinning too fast for her to ride along, but his kiss kept her centered in the midst of the tornado of sensation. She wrapped her arms around his neck, her breathing ragged.

He kissed her then, his mouth hot, insistent, demanding. That was all it took. With a sharp cry, she let go of what tiny tendrils of control remained and flung herself into the whirling, breathtaking maelstrom.

Even before the last delicious tremors had faded, he produced a condom from his wallet and entered her with one swift movement.

Long unused muscles stretched to welcome him and he groaned, pressing his forehead to hers.

"So tight," he murmured.

"I'm sorry."

His laugh was rough and tickled her skin. "I don't believe I was complaining."

He kissed her fiercely, possessively, and just like that, she could feel her body rise to meet his again.

With her hands gripped tightly in his, he moved inside her and she arched restlessly against him, her body seeking more, burning for completion. And then she could sense a change in him, feel the taut edginess in every touch. Her mouth tangled with his and at the slick brush of his tongue against hers, she climaxed again, with a core-deep sigh of delight.

He froze above her, his muscles corded, and then he groaned and joined her in the storm.

He came back to earth with a powerful sense of the surreal. None of this seemed to be truly happening. Not the hard floor beneath his shoulders or the soft, warm curves in his arms or this unaccustomed contentment stealing through him.

It was definitely genuine, though. He could feel her pulse against his arm where her head lay nestled and smell that delectable scent of her.

"How could I have forgotten?" she murmured.

He angled his head to better see her expression. "Forgotten what?"

She smiled and he was struck again by her breathtaking beauty. She was like some rare, exquisite flower that bloomed in secret just for him.

"This radiant feeling. Total contentment. As if for a few short moments, everything is perfect in the world."

He smiled, enchanted by her. "You don't think everything would be a tad more perfect if we happened to be in a soft bed somewhere instead of on the bare floor of your ripped-apart spare room? I think I've got paint chips in places I'm not sure I should mention."

She made a face, though he saw laughter dancing in her eyes. "Go ahead. Ruin the moment for me."

"Sorry. It's just been a long time since I've been so…carried away."

"I know exactly what you mean."

He studied her. "How long?"

Her lovely green-eyed gaze met his, then flickered away. "Since the night before Scott's accident. So that would be eight years, if anyone's counting."

"In all that time, not once?"

As soon as his shocked words escaped, he realized they weren't very tactful, but she didn't seem offended.

"I loved my husband," she said solemnly. "Even if he wasn't quite the man I expected to spend the rest of my life with when I married him, I loved him and I honored my wedding vows."

He pulled her closer, stunned at her loyalty and devotion. She had put her life, her future, completely on hold for years to care for a man who could never be the sort of husband a young woman needed.

Most women he knew would have felt perfectly justified in resuming their own lives after such a tragic accident. They might have mourned their husband for a while but would have been quick to put the past behind them.

He thought of his own mother, selfish and feckless, who wasn't happy unless she was the center of attention. She wouldn't have had the first idea how to cope after such a tragedy.

Not Tess. She had stayed, had sacrificed her youth for her husband.

"Scott was an incredibly fortunate man to have you."

Her eyes softened. "Thank you, Quinn." She kissed him gently, her mouth warm and soft, and he was astonished at the fragile tenderness that fluttered through him like dry leaves on the autumn wind.

"Can I stay?" he asked. "It's…harder than I expected to hang out at the ranch right now."

She smiled against his mouth and her kiss left no question in his mind about what her answer would be.

"Of course. I would love you to stay. And I even have a bed in the other room, believe it or not."

He rose and pulled her to her feet, stunned all over again at the peace welling inside him. He didn't think he had come here for this on a conscious level, but perhaps some part of him knew she would welcome him, would soothe the ache in his heart with that easy nurturing that was such a part of her.

"Show me," he murmured.

Her smile was brilliant and took his breath away as she took him by the hand and led him from the room.

* * *

She was having a torrid affair.

Two days later, Tess could hardly believe it, even when the evidence was sprawled beside her, wide shoulders propped against her headboard, looking rugged and masculine against the dainty yellow frills and flowers of her bedroom.

The fluffy comforter on her bed covered him to the waist and she found the contrast between the feminine fabric and the hard planes and hollows of his muscled chest infinitely arousing.

She sighed softly, wondering if she would ever get tired of looking at him, touching him, laughing with him.

For two days, they hadn't left her house, except for sneaking in one quick trip to Winder Ranch in the middle of the night for him to grab some extra clothes and toiletries.

What would the rest of the town think if news spread that the sainted Tess Claybourne was engaged in a wild, torrid relationship with Quinn Southerland, the former bad boy of Pine Gulch?

Enthusiastically engaged, no less. She flushed at the memory of her response to him, of the heat and magic and connection they had shared the past few days. The sensual, passionate woman she had become in his arms seemed like a stranger, as if she had stored up all these feelings and desires inside her through the past eight years.

She didn't know whether to be embarrassed or thrilled that she had discovered this part of herself with him.

"You're blushing," he said now with an interested look. "What are you thinking about?"

"You. This. I was thinking about how I had no idea I could...that we could..."

Her voice trailed off as she struggled with words to finish the sentence. Her own discomfort astounded her. How could she possibly possess even a hint of awkwardness after everything they had done together within these walls, all the secrets they had shared?

He didn't seem to need any explanation.

"You absolutely can. And we absolutely have."

He grinned, looking male and gorgeous and so completely content with the world that she couldn't help laughing.

This was the other thing that shocked her, that she could have such fun with him. He wasn't at all the intense, brooding rebel she had thought when they were younger. Quinn had a sly sense of humor and a keen sense of the ridiculous.

They laughed about everything from a silly horror movie they watched on TV in the middle of the night to the paint flecks in her hair after they made one halfhearted attempt to continue working on the trim in the guest room to a phone call from Easton the day before, wondering if Tess had kidnapped him.

And they had talked, endlessly. About his memories of the other Four Winds, about growing up on the ranch, about her friends and family and the miracle of how she had been led to become a nurse long before Scott's accident when those skills would become so vital.

They had also talked a great deal about his foster mother and also about Guff. He seemed to find great comfort in sharing memories with her. That he would trust her with those memories touched and warmed her, more than she could ever express. She hoped his sorrow eased a little as he brought those events and people to life for her.

"I wish it didn't have to end," she murmured now, then wished she could recall the words.

No regrets, she had promised herself that first night. She intended only to seize every ounce of happiness she could with him and then let him go with a glad heart that she had this chance to share a few wonderful days with him.

He traced a hand along her bare arm. "I wish I could put off my return to Seattle. But I've been away too long as it is. My plane's coming tomorrow."

"I know."

Her smile felt tight, forced, as she fought to hide the sadness hovering just out of reach at his impending departure.

How had he become so very important to her in just a few short weeks? Even the idea of moving to Portland, starting over with new friends and different employment challenges, had lost much of its luster.

Ridiculous, she told herself. She couldn't let herself fall into a funk over the inevitable end of a passionate, albeit brief, affair, even one with the man who had fascinated her for two decades.

"We should do something," he said suddenly.

She took in the rumpled bedclothes and the hard muscles of his bare chest. "I thought we *had* been doing something."

His sensual smile just about took her breath away. "I meant go to dinner or something. It's not fair for me to keep you chained up in the bedroom for two days without even offering to feed you."

"We haven't tried the chained-up thing."

"Yet."

Her insides shivered at the single word in that low growl of a voice.

"We could go to The Gulch," he suggested, apparently unaffected by the same sudden vivid fantasies that flashed across her mind.

She pushed them away, wondering what the regulars or Lou and Donna Archeleta would think if she showed up in the café with Quinn looking rumpled and well-loved. What did she care? She thought. She deserved some happiness and fun in her life and if she found that with Quinn, it was nobody's damn business but theirs.

"What about the others?" she asked. "Easton and Brant and Cisco? Don't you think you ought to spend your last night in town with them?"

He made a face, though she thought he looked struck by the reminder of his friends and the shared loss that had brought them all together.

"I should," he finally admitted. "I stayed an extra few days after the funeral to spend time with them but I ended up a little…distracted."

She pulled away from him and slipped her arms through her robe. "I should never have monopolized all your time."

"It was a mutual monopoly. I wanted to be here."

"If you want to spend your last evening at the ranch with them, please don't feel you can't because of me. Because of this."

"Why do I have to choose? We should all go to dinner together."

She frowned. "I'm not one of you, Quinn."

"After the past two weeks, you feel as much a part of the family as any of us."

She wanted to argue that the others would probably want him to themselves and she couldn't blame them. But she had discovered she had a selfish streak hiding inside her. She couldn't give up the chance to spend at least a few more hours with him.

Chapter Thirteen

In her heart, Tess knew she didn't belong here with the others but she couldn't remember an evening she had enjoyed more.

Several hours later, she sat at the table in the Winder Ranch dining room and sipped at her wine, listening to the flow of conversation eddy around her.

When they weren't teasing Easton about something, they were reminiscing about some camping trip Guff took them on into Yellowstone or the moose that chased them once along the shores of Hayden Lake or snow-mobiling into the high country.

In every word and gesture, it was obvious they loved each other deeply, despite a few rough moments in the conversation.

Most notably, something was definitely up between

Easton and Cisco, Tess thought. Though outwardly Easton treated him just as she did Brant and Quinn, with a sisterly sort of affection, Tess could sense braided ropes of tension tugging between the two of them.

They sat on opposite sides of the table and Easton was careful to avoid looking at him for very long.

What was it? she wondered. Had they fought about something? She had a feeling this wasn't something recent in origin as she remembered Easton's strange reaction whenever Cisco's name had been mentioned, before he made it back to the ranch. Obviously, her feelings were different for him than for Brant and Quinn and Tess wondered if anybody else but her was aware of it.

They all seemed so different to her and yet it was obvious they were a unit. Easton, who loved the ranch and was the only one of the Four Winds not to wander away from it. Brant, the solemn, honorable soldier who seemed to be struggling with internal demons she couldn't begin to guess at. Cisco, who by his demeanor appeared to be a thrill-seeking adventurer type, though she sensed there was much more to him than he revealed.

And then there was Quinn.

Around the others, these three people who were his closest friends and the only family he had left, he was warm and affectionate as they laughed and talked and shared memories and she was enthralled by him all over again.

She was the odd person out but Quinn had insisted she join them, even after Easton suggested they grill steaks at the ranch instead of going out to dinner.

The ranch house seemed empty without Jo. She wondered how Easton endured it—and how her friend would cope when she was alone here at the ranch after the men went their respective ways once more.

"Do you remember that snow prank?" Cisco said with a laugh. "That was classic, man. A masterpiece."

"I still can't believe you guys drove all the way into Idaho Falls just to rent a fake snow machine," Easton said, still not looking at Cisco.

"Hey, I tried to talk them out of it," Brant defended himself.

Quinn gave a rough laugh. "But you still drove the getaway car after we broke into the gymnasium and sprayed the Sweetheart Dance decorations with six inches of fake snow."

Tess set down her fork and narrowed her gaze at the men. "Wait a minute. That was you?"

"Uh-oh. You are so busted." Easton grinned at Quinn.

"I worked on that dance planning committee for weeks! I can't believe you would be so blatantly destructive."

"We were just trying to help out with the theme," Quinn said. "Wasn't it something about snuggling in with your sweetheart for Valentine's Day? What better time to snuggle than in the middle of a blizzard and six inches of snow?"

She gave him a mock glare. "Nice try."

"It was a long time ago. I say we all forgive and forget," Brant said, winking at Tess.

"Do you have any idea how long it takes to clean up six inches of snow from a high-school gymnasium?"

"Hey, blame it all on Quinn. I was an innocent sophomore he dragged along for the ride," Cisco said with a grin.

"You were never innocent," Easton muttered.

He sent her a quick look out of hooded dark eyes. "True enough."

Tess could feel the tension sizzle between them, though the other two men seemed oblivious to it. She wondered if any of them saw the anguished expression in Easton's eyes as she watched Cisco.

The other woman suddenly shoved her chair away from the table. "Anybody up for dessert?" she asked, a falsely bright note to her voice. "Jenna McRaven owed me a favor so I talked her into making some of her famous turtle cheesecake."

"That would be great," Brant said. "Thank you."

"Quinn? Cisco?"

Both men readily agreed and Easton headed for the kitchen.

"I'll help," Tess offered, sliding her chair away from the table. "But don't think I've forgotten the snow prank. As to forgiving, I don't believe there's a statute of limitations on prosecution for breaking the spirit of the high-school dance committee."

All three of the men laughed as she left the room, apparently unfazed by her empty threat.

In the kitchen, she found Easton reaching into the refrigerator. She emerged holding a delectable-looking dessert drizzled in chocolate and caramel and chopped nuts.

"All right, out with it," Easton said as she set the cheesecake on the counter, and Tess realized this was the first chance they'd had all evening to speak privately.

"With what?" Tess asked in as innocent a voice as she could muster, though she had a feeling she sounded no more innocent than Cisco had.

"You and Quinn. He's been gone from the ranch for two entire days! What's going on with you two?"

She turned pink, remembering the passion and fun of the past two days.

"Nothing. Not really. We're just… He's just…"

"You're right. It's none of my business," Easton said as she sliced the cheesecake and began transferring it to serving plates. "Sorry I asked."

"It's not that, I just… I can't really explain it."

Easton was silent for a long moment. "Are you sure you know what you're dealing with when it comes to Quinn?" she finally asked with a searching look. "I wouldn't be a friend if I didn't ask."

"He's leaving tomorrow. I completely understand that."

"Do you?"

Tess nodded, even as her heart gave a sad little twist. "Of course. These past few days have been…magical, but I know it's only temporary. His life is in Seattle. Mine is here, at least for the next few weeks until I move to Portland."

"Seattle and Portland aren't so far apart that you couldn't connect if you wanted to," Easton pointed out.

She wouldn't think about that, especially after she had worked so hard to convince herself their relationship was only temporary, born out of shared grief and stunning, surprising hunger.

"I care about you," Easton said when Tess didn't answer. "We owe you so much for these past weeks with Aunt Jo. You carried all of us through it. I mean that, Tess. You always knew exactly what to say and what to do, no matter what was happening, and I'll be forever grateful to you for all you did for her. That's why I'll be absolutely furious if Quinn takes advantage of your natural compassion and ends up hurting you."

"He won't. I promise."

Easton didn't look convinced. Not surprising, she supposed, since Tess couldn't even manage to convince herself.

"It's just…he doesn't have a great track record when it comes to women," her friend said quietly.

Tess tried hard to make her sudden fierce interest in that particular subject seem casual. "Really?"

"I love him like a brother and have since he came to the ranch. But I'm not blind to his faults, especially when it comes to women. I don't think Quinn has ever had a relationship that has lasted longer than a few weeks. To be honest, I'm not sure he's capable of it."

"Never?"

"I can't be certain, I suppose. He's been away for a long time. But every time I ask about his social life when we talk on the phone or e-mail, he mentions he's dating someone new."

"Maybe he just hasn't met anyone he wants to get serious with. There's nothing wrong with that."

"I think it's more than that, Tess. If I had to guess, I would assume it has something to do with his parents' marriage. He didn't have an easy childhood and I think it's made him gun-shy about relationships and commitment."

"I'm sure it did. He told me about his parents and his messed-up home life."

Surprise flashed in her blue eyes. "He did?"

She nodded. "It can't be easy getting past something like that."

"When we were kids, he vowed over and over that

he was never going to get married. To be honest, judging by his track record, I don't think he's changed his mind one bit. It broke Jo's heart, if you want the truth. She wanted to see us all settled before she died, but that didn't happen, did it?"

Tess forced a smile, though the cracks in her own heart widened a little more. "Easton, it's okay. I'm not interested in something long-term right now with Quinn or anyone else. We both needed…peace for a while after Jo's death and we enjoy each other's company. That's all there is to it."

Easton didn't look at all convinced and Tess decided to change the uncomfortable subject.

"What time does Cisco leave tomorrow?" she asked.

The diversion worked exactly as she hoped. Easton's expression of concern slid into something else entirely, something stark and painful.

"A few hours." Her hand shook a little as she set the last slice of cheesecake on a small serving plate. "He's catching a plane out of Salt Lake City to Central America at noon tomorrow, so he'll be leaving in the early hours of the morning."

Tess covered her hand and Easton gave her an anguished look.

"Without Jo here, I don't know if he'll ever come back. Or Quinn, for that matter. Brant at least has his own ranch up the canyon so I'm sure I'll at least see him occasionally. But the other two…" Her voice trailed off. "Nothing will be the same without Aunt Jo."

Tess pulled Easton into a hug. "It won't be the same," she agreed. "But you're still here. They'll come back for you."

"I don't know about that."

"They will." Tess gave her friend a little shake. "Anyway, Jo would be the first one to tell you to seize every moment. They might not be back for a while but they're here now. Don't sour the joy you can find tonight with them by stewing about what might be coming tomorrow."

"You must be channeling Jo now. I can almost hear her in my head saying exactly those same words."

"Then you'd better listen." Tess smiled.

Easton sighed. "We'd better get this cheesecake out there before they come looking for us."

"Can you give me a minute? I need some water, but I'll be right out."

Easton gave her a searching look. "Are you sure you're all right?"

Tess forced a smile. "Of course. You've got three men waiting for dessert out there. You'd better hurry."

After a pause, Easton nodded and carried the tray with the cheesecake slices out to the dining room.

When she was alone in the bright, cheery kitchen, Tess leaned against the counter and fought the urge to cover her face with her hands and weep.

She was a terrible liar. Lucky for her, Easton was too wrapped up in her own troubles to pay close attention.

She absolutely *wasn't* okay, and she had a sinking feeling she wouldn't be for a long, long time.

I'm not interested in something long-term right now with Quinn or anyone else.

It was a wonder Jo didn't rise up and smite her for telling such a blatant fib in the middle of her kitchen.

Finally, she admitted to herself the truth she had been

fighting for two days. Longer, probably. The truth that had been hovering just on the edges of her subconscious.

She was in love with him.

With Quinn Southerland, who planned to blow out of her life like the south wind in the morning.

She loved the way his mouth quirked up at the edge when he teased her about something. She loved his tender care of Jo in her final days and his deep appreciation of the family and home he had found here. She loved the strength and honor that had carried him through incredible trauma as a boy.

She loved the way he made her feel, cherished and beautiful and *wanted,* and the heat and abandon she experienced in his arms.

And she especially loved that he knew the very worst parts of her and wanted to spend time with her anyway.

Whatever was she going to do without him in her world? Just the thought of going through the motions after he returned to Seattle left her achy and heartsore.

She knew she would survive. What other choice did she have?

That didn't mean she wanted to. Hadn't she faced enough heartache? Just once in her life, couldn't things work out the way she wanted?

Fighting back a sob, she moved to the sink and poured a glass of water so she could convince herself she hadn't completely prevaricated to Easton.

She thought of her advice to her friend a few moments earlier.

Don't sour the joy you can find in today by stewing about what might be coming tomorrow.

She couldn't ruin these last few hours with him by anticipating the pain she knew waited for her around the corner.

Something was wrong.

He never claimed to be the most perceptive of men when it came to the opposite sex, but even *he* could tell Tess was distracted and troubled after dinner when he drove her back from the ranch to town.

She said little, mostly gazed out the window at the lights flickering in the darkness, few and far between in Cold Creek Canyon and becoming more concentrated as he approached the town limits.

He glanced over at her profile, thinking how serenely lovely she was. He supposed her pensiveness was rubbing off on him because he still couldn't quite process the surreal twist his life had taken these past few days.

If Brant or Cisco—or Easton, even—had told him before he came back to town that he would wrap up his visit to Pine Gulch in Tess Jamison Claybourne's bed, he would have thought it was some kind of a strange, twisted joke.

Until he showed up at the ranch a few weeks ago, he honestly hadn't thought of her much in years. He was too busy working his tail off building his business to waste much time or energy on such an unimportant—though undeniably aggravating—part of his past.

On the rare occasions when thoughts of her did filter through his mind for whatever reason, they were usually tainted with acrimony and disdain.

In these past weeks, she had become so much more to him.

Quinn let out a breath. He had tried to avoid examining those fragile, tender feelings too carefully. He appreciated her care for Jo, admired the strength she had demonstrated through her own personal tragedy, found her incredibly sexy.

He didn't want to poke and prod more deeply than that, afraid to unravel the tangled mess of his feelings.

He did know he didn't want to leave her or the haven he had found in her arms.

His hands tightened on the steering wheel as he turned down the street toward her house. For two weeks, his associates had taken the helm of Southerland Shipping. Quinn ought to be ecstatic at the idea of jumping right back into the middle of the action. Strategizing, making decisions, negotiating contracts. It was all in his blood, the one thing he found he was good at, and he had certainly missed the work while he had been at Winder Ranch.

But every time he thought about saying goodbye to Tess, he started to feel restless and uneasy and he had no idea why.

He pulled into the driveway and turned off the engine to his rented SUV.

"You probably want to be with the others," she said, her voice low. "I don't mind if we say goodbye now."

Something remarkably like panic fluttered through him. "Are you that anxious to be rid of me?"

She turned wide green eyes toward him. "No. Nothing like that! I just… I assumed you would want to spend your last few hours in town with your friends," she said, a vulnerable note to her voice that shocked him.

Though he had already said his farewells to the others

when he left the house, with lots of hugs and backslapping, he considered taking the out she was offering him. Maybe he ought to just gather his few belongings from her house and head back to bunk at the ranch for the night. That made perfect sense and would help him begin the process of rebuilding all those protective walls around his emotions.

But he had a few more hours in Pine Gulch and he couldn't bear the thought of leaving her yet.

"I'd like to stay."

He said the words as more of a question than a statement. After an endless moment when he was quite certain she was going to tell him to hit the road, she nodded, much to his vast relief, and reached for his hand.

A soft, terrifying sweetness unfurled inside him at the touch of her hand in his.

How was he going to walk away in a few hours from this woman who had in a few short weeks become so vitally important to him? He didn't have the first idea.

Chapter Fourteen

She didn't release his hand, even as she unlocked her door to let them both inside. When he closed the door behind him, she kissed him with a fierce, almost desperate, hunger.

They didn't even make it past her living room, clawing at clothes, ripping at buttons, tangling mouths with a fiery passion that stunned him.

They had made love in a dozen different ways over the past few days—easy, teasing, urgent, soft.

But never with this explosive heat that threatened to consume them both. She climaxed the instant he entered her and he groaned as her body pulsed around him and followed her just seconds later.

He kissed her, trying to memorize every taste and texture as she clutched him tightly to her. To his amazement, after just a few moments, his body started to stir again inside her and he could feel by her response that she was becoming aroused again.

He carried her to the bedroom and took enough time to undress both of them, wondering if he would ever get enough of her silky curves and the warm, sweet welcome of her body.

This time was slow, tender, with an edge of poignancy to it that made his chest ache. Did she sense it, too? he wondered.

They tasted and touched for a long time, until both of them were breathless, boneless. She cried out his name when she climaxed and he thought she said something else against his shoulder but he couldn't understand the words.

When he could breathe again and manage to string together two semi-coherent thoughts, he pulled her close under the crook of his arm, memorizing the feel of her— the curves and hollows, the soft delight of her skin.

"I wish I didn't have to go," he murmured again.

Instead of smiling or perhaps expressing the same regret, she froze in his arms and then pulled away.

Though her bedroom was well-heated against the October chill, he was instantly cold, as he watched her slip her slender arms through the sleeves of her silky green robe that matched her eyes.

"Are you lying for my sake or to appease your own guilt?" she finally asked him.

He blinked, disoriented at the rapid-fire shift from tender and passionate to this unexpected attack that instantly set him on the defensive.

"Why do I have to be lying?"

"Come on, Quinn," she said, her voice almost sad. "We both know you're not sorry. Not really."

He bristled. "When did you become such an expert on what's going on inside my head?"

"I could never claim such omnipotent power. Nor would I want it."

Okay. He absolutely did not understand how a woman's mind worked. How could she pick a fight with him after the incredible intensity they just shared? Was she just trying to make their inevitable parting easier?

"If you could see inside my head," he answered carefully, "you would see I meant every word. I *do* wish I didn't have so many obligations waiting for me back in Seattle. These past few days have been…peaceful and I don't have much of that in my life."

She gazed at him, her features tight with an expression he didn't recognize. After a moment, her prickly mood seemed to slide away and she smiled, though it didn't quite push away that strange, almost bereft look in her eyes.

"I'm happy for that, Quinn. You deserve a little peace in your life and I'm glad you found it here."

She paused and looked away from him. "But we both knew from the beginning that this would never be anything but temporary."

Whenever he let himself think beyond the wonder of the moment, the shared laughter and unexpected joy he found with her, he had assumed exactly that—this was supposed to be a short-term relationship that wouldn't extend beyond these few magical days.

Hearing the words from her somehow made the reality seem more bluntly desolate.

"Does it have to be?"

"Of course," she answered briskly. "What other option is there?"

He told himself that wasn't hurt churning through him at her dismissal of all they had shared and at the potential for them to share more.

"Portland is only a few hours from Seattle. We could certainly still see each other on the weekends."

She tightened the sash on her robe with fingers that seemed to tremble slightly. From the cold? he wondered. Or from something else?

"To what end?" she asked. "Great sex and amusing conversation?"

Despite his turmoil, he couldn't resist arching an eyebrow. "Something wrong with either of those?"

Her laugh sounded rough. "Not at all. Believe me, I've become a big fan of both these past few days."

She shoved her hands in the pockets of her robe and drew in a deep breath, as if steeling herself for unpleasantness. "But I'm afraid neither is enough for me."

That edgy disquiet from earlier returned in full force and he was aware of a pitiful impulse to beg her not to push him from her life.

He wouldn't, though. He had a sudden, ugly flashback of his mother at the dinner table trying desperately to catch his father's attention any way she could. New earrings, new silverware, a difficult new recipe. Only until she managed to push one of his father's hot buttons would he even notice her, and then only to rant and rail and sometimes worse.

He pushed it away. He certainly wasn't his mother trying desperately in her own sick way to make someone care who wasn't really capable of it. Tess was not like his father. She had a deep capacity for love. He had seen it with Jo, even Easton and Brant and Cisco.

Why else would she have stayed with an invalid husband for so long?

But maybe she couldn't care for *him*. Maybe he didn't deserve someone like her....

"I want more," she said quietly, interrupting the grim direction of his thoughts. "All I wanted when I was a girl was a home and a family and a husband who cherished me. I wanted what my parents had. They held hands in the movies and whispered secrets to each other in restaurants and hid love notes for each other all around the house. My mom's still finding them, years after Dad died. That's what I wanted."

He was silent. If not for the years he spent with Jo and Guff seeing just that sort of relationship, he would have had absolutely no frame of reference to understand what she was talking about, but the Winders had shared a love like that, deep and rich and genuine.

"I thought I found that with Scott," Tess went on, "but fate had other plans and things didn't turn out quite the way I dreamed."

"I'm sorry." He meant the words. He hated thinking of her enduring such loss and pain as a young bride.

"I'm sorry, too," she said quietly. "But that time in my life is over. I'm ready to move forward now."

"I can understand that. But why can't you move forward with me? We have something good here. You know we do."

She was silent for a long time and he thought perhaps

he was making progress on getting her to see his point of view. But when she spoke, her voice was low and sad.

"Easton told me tonight that when you were younger, you vowed you were never getting married."

"What a guy says when he's fifteen and what he says when he's thirty-four are two very different things," he said, though he had said that very same sentiment to Jo in the garden at Winder Ranch just a few weeks ago.

She sat on the bed and he didn't miss the way she was careful to keep plenty of space between them. "Okay, tell me the truth. Say we continue to see each other for those weekends you were talking about. Look ahead several months, maybe a year, with a few days a month of more of that great sex and amusing conversation."

"I can do that," he said, and spent several very pleasant seconds imagining kissing her on the dock of his house on Mercer Island, of taking her up in his boat for a quick run to Victoria, of standing beside the ocean on the Oregon Coast at a wonderfully romantic boutique hotel he knew in Cannon Beach.

"So here it is a year in the future," she said, dousing his hazy fantasies like a cold surf. "Say we've seen each other exclusively for that time and have come to…to care about each other. Where do you see things going from there?"

"I don't know. What do you want me to see?"

"Marriage. Family. Can you ever even imagine yourself contemplating a forever sort of relationship with me or anyone else?"

Marriage. Kids. A dog. Panic spurted through him. Though Jo and Guff had shared a good marriage and he had spent a few years watching their example, for most of his childhood, marriage had meant cold silences alternated with screaming fights and tantrums, culminating in terrible violence that had changed his world forever.

"Maybe," he managed to say after a moment. "Who's to say? That would be a long way in the future. Why do we have to jump from here to there in an instant?"

Her sigh was heavy, almost sad. "I saw that panic in your eyes, Quinn. You can't even consider the idea of it in some long-distant future without being spooked."

"That could change. I don't see why we have to ruin this. Why can't we just enjoy what we have in the moment?"

She didn't answer him right away. "You know, brain injuries are peculiar, unpredictable things," she finally said, baffling him with the seemingly random shift in topic.

"Are they?"

"The same injury in the same spot can affect two people in completely different ways. For the first two or three years after Scott's accident, all the doctors and specialists kept telling me not to give up hope, that things would get better. He could still improve and start regaining function some day."

Through his confusion, Quinn's heart always ached when he thought of Tess facing all that on her own.

"I waited and hoped and prayed," she went on. "Through all those years and promises, I felt as if I were frozen in the moment, that the world went on while I was stuck in place, waiting for something that never happened."

She paused. "He did improve, in minuscule ways. I don't want you to think he didn't. Near the end, he could hold his head up for long periods of time and even started laughing at my silly jokes again. But it was not nearly the recovery I dreamed about in those early days."

"Tess, I'm very sorry you went through that. But I don't understand your point."

She swallowed and didn't meet his gaze. "My point is that I spent years waiting for reality to match up to my expectations, waiting for him to change. Even being angry when those expectations weren't met, when in truth, he simply wasn't capable of it. It wasn't his fault. Just the way things were."

He stared. "So you're comparing me to someone who was critically brain-injured in a car accident?"

She sighed. "Not at all, Quinn. I'm talking about myself. One of the greatest lessons Scott's accident taught me was pragmatism. I can't hang on to unrealistic dreams and hopes anymore. I want marriage and children and you don't. It's as simple as that."

"Does it have to be?"

"For me, yes. Your views might change. I hope for your sake they do. Caring for Scott all those years taught me that the only way we can really find purpose and meaning in life is if we somehow manage to move outside ourselves to embrace the chances we're offered to care for someone else."

She lifted moist eyes to his. "I hope you change your mind, Quinn. But what if you don't? Say we see each other for six months or a year and then you decide you're still no closer to shifting your perspective about home and family. I would have spent another year moving further away from my dreams. I can't do that to myself or to you."

That panic from before churned through him, icy and sharp. He didn't want to lose what they had shared these past few days.

Or maybe it didn't mean as much to her. Why else would she be so willing to throw it all away? Maybe he *was* just like his mother, trying desperately to keep her from pushing him away.

No. This wasn't about that. The fear and panic warring inside him took on an edge of anger.

"This is it, then?" His voice turned hard, ugly. "I was here to scratch an itch for you and now you're shoving me out the door."

Her lovely features paled. "Not fair."

"Fair? Don't talk to me about fair." He jumped out of the bed and reached for his Levis, still in a heap on the floor. He couldn't seem to stop the ugly words from spilling out like toxic effluent.

"You know what I just realized? You haven't changed a bit since your days as Queen Bee at Pine Gulch High. You're still the spoiled, manipulative girl you were in high school. You want what you want and to hell with anybody else and whatever they might need."

"This has nothing to do with high school or the person I was back then."

"Wrong. This has *everything* to do with Tess Jamison, Homecoming Queen. You can't have what you want, your little fantasy happily-ever-after, and so kicking me out of your life completely is your version of throwing a pissy little temper tantrum."

His gazed narrowed as another repugnant thought occurred to him.

"Or wait. Maybe that's not it at all. Maybe this is all

some manipulative trick, the kind you used to be so very good. Don't forget, I had years of experience watching you bat your eyes at some poor idiot, all the while you're tightening the noose around his neck without him having the first clue what you're doing. Maybe you think if you push me out now, in a few weeks I'll come running back with tears and apologies, ready to give you anything you want. Even that all-important wedding ring that's apparently the only thing you think matters."

"You're being ridiculous."

"You forget, I was the chief recipient of all those dirty tricks you perfected in high school. The lies. The rumors you spread. This is just one more trick, isn't it? Well, guess what? I'm not playing your games now, anymore than I was willing to do it back then."

She stood on the other side of the room now, her arms folded across her chest and hurt and anger radiating from her.

"You can't get past it, can you?" She shook her head. "I have apologized and tried to show you I'm a different person than I was then. But you refuse to even consider the possibility that I might have changed."

He had considered it. He had even believed it for a while.

"Only one of us is stuck in the past, Quinn. Life has changed me and given me a new perspective. But somewhere deep inside you, you're still a boy stuck in the ugliness of his parents' marriage."

He stared at her, angry that she would turn this all back around on him when she was the one being a manipulative bitch.

"You're crazy."

"Am I? I think the reason you won't let yourself have more than casual relationships with women is because you're so determined not to turn into either one of your parents. You're not about to become your powerless, emotionally needy mother or your workaholic, abusive father. So you've decided somewhere deep in your psyche that your best bet is to just keep everyone else at arm's length so you don't have to risk either option."

He was so furious, he couldn't think straight. Her assessment was brutal and harsh and he refused to admit that it might also be true.

"Now you're some kind of armchair psychiatrist?"

"No. Just a woman who…cares about you, Quinn."

"You've got a hell of a way of showing it by pushing me away."

"I'm not pushing you away." Her voice shook and he saw tears in her eyes. Either she was a much better actress than he could possibly imagine or that was genuine regret in her eyes. He didn't know which to believe.

"You have no idea how hard this is for me," she said and one of those tears trickled down the side of her nose. "I've come to care about you these past few weeks. Maybe I always did, a little. But as much as I have loved these past few days and part of me wants nothing more than to continue seeing you after I move to Portland, it wouldn't be fair to either of us. You can't be the kind of man I want and I'm afraid I would eventually come to hate you for that."

His arms ached from the effort it took not to reach for her but he kept his hands fisted at his sides. "So that's it. See you later, thanks for the good time in the sack and all that."

"If you want to be crude about it."

He didn't. He wanted to grab her and hang on tight and tell her he would be whatever kind of man she wanted him to be. He had discovered a safety, a serenity, with her he hadn't found anywhere else and the idea of leaving it behind left him hollow and achy.

But she was right. He couldn't offer her the things she needed. He could lie and tell her otherwise but both of them would see through it and end up even more unhappy.

"I suppose there's nothing left to say, then, is there?"

She released a shuddering kind of breath and he supposed he should be somewhat mollified that her eyes reflected the same kind of pain shredding his insides.

"I'm sorry."

"So am I, Tess."

He grabbed his things and walked out the door, hoping despite himself that she would call him back, tell him she didn't mean anything she'd said.

But the only sound as he climbed into his rental car was the mournful October wind in the trees and the distant howl of a coyote.

Tess stood at the window of her bedroom watching Quinn's taillights disappear into the night.

She couldn't seem to catch her breath and she felt as if she'd just been bucked off one of the Winder Ranch horses, then kicked in the chest for good measure.

Had she been wrong? Maybe she should have just taken whatever crumbs Quinn could offer, to hell with the inevitable pain she knew waited for her in some murky future.

At least then she wouldn't have this raw, devastating feeling that she had just made a terrible mistake.

With great effort, she forced herself to draw in a deep breath and then another and another, willing her common sense to override the visceral pain and vast emptiness gaping inside her.

No. She hadn't been wrong, as much as she might wish otherwise. In the deep corners of her heart, she knew it.

She wanted a home and a family. Not today, maybe not even next year, but someday, certainly. She was ready to move forward with her life and go on to the next stage.

She had already fallen in love with him, just from these few days. If she spent a year of those weekend encounters he was talking about, she wasn't sure she would ever be able to climb back out.

Better to break things off now, when she at least had half a chance of repairing the shattered pieces of her heart.

She would survive. She had been through worse. Scott's death and the long, difficult years preceding it had taught her she had hidden reservoirs of strength.

She supposed that was a good thing. She had a feeling she was going to need all the strength she could find in the coming months as she tried to go on without Quinn.

Chapter Fifteen

"Tess? Everything okay?"

Three months after Jo Winder's death, Tess stood at the nurses' station, a chart in her hand and her mind a million miles away.

Or at least several hundred.

She jerked her mind away from Pine Gulch and the tangled mess she had made of things and looked up to find her friend and charge nurse watching her with concern in her brown eyes.

"I'm fine," she answered Vicki Ballantine.

"Are you sure? You look white as a sheet and you've been standing there for at least five minutes without moving a muscle. Come sit down, honey, and have a sip of water."

The older woman tugged her toward one of the chairs

behind the long blue desk. Since Vicki was not only her friend but technically her boss, Tess didn't feel as if she had a great deal of choice.

She sipped at the water and crushed ice Vicki brought her in a foam cup. It did seem to quell the nausea a little, though it didn't do much for the panic that seemed to pound a steady drumbeat through her.

"You want to tell me what's bothering you?" Vicki asked.

She drew in a breath then let it out slowly, still reeling from confirmation of what she had begun to suspect for a few weeks but had only just confirmed an hour ago on her lunch break.

This sudden upheaval all seemed so surreal, the last possible development she had expected to disrupt everything.

"I don't… I haven't been sleeping well."

Vicki leaned on the edge of the deck, her plump features set into a frown. "You're settling in okay, aren't you? The house you rented is nice enough, right? It's in a quiet neighborhood."

"Yes. Everything's fine. I love Portland, you know I do. The house is great and everyone here at the hospital has been wonderful."

"But you're still not happy."

At the gentle concern in her friend's eyes and the warm touch of her hand squeezing Tess's arms, tears welled up in her eyes.

"I am," she lied. "I'm just…"

She couldn't finish the sentence as those tears spilled over. She pressed her hands to her eyes, mortified that she was breaking down at work.

Only the hormones, she assured herself, but she knew it was much, much more. Her tears stemmed from fear and longing and the emptiness in her heart that kept her tossing and turning all night.

Vicki took one look at her emotional reaction and pulled Tess back to her feet, this time ushering her into the privacy of the empty nurses' lounge.

"All right. Out with it. Tell Auntie Vick what's wrong. This is about some man, isn't it?"

Through her tears, Tess managed a watery laugh. "You could say that."

Oh, she had made such a snarled mess of everything. That panic pulsed through her again, harsh and unforgiving, and her thoughts pulsed with it.

"It always is," Vicki said with a knowing look. "Funny thing is, I didn't even know you were dating anybody."

"I'm not. We're…" Her voice trailed off and she drew in a heavy breath. Though she wanted to protect her own privacy and give herself time to sort things out, she was also desperate to share the information with *someone*.

She couldn't call her mother. Oh, mercy, there was another reason for panic. What would Maura say?

Her mother wasn't here and she wasn't anywhere close to ready to tell any of her friends in Pine Gulch. Vicki had become her closest friend since moving to Portland and on impulse, she decided she could trust her.

"I'm pregnant," she blurted out.

Vicki's eyes widened in shock and her mouth made a perfect little *O* for a moment before she shut it with a snap. She said nothing for several long moments.

Just when Tess was kicking herself for even mentioning it in the first place, Vicki gave her a careful look. "And how do you feel about that?"

"You're the one who said I'm pale as a sheet, right? That's probably a pretty good indication."

"Your color's coming back but you still look upset."

"I don't know how I feel yet, to tell you the truth," she admitted. "I just went to the doctor on my lunch hour to verify my suspicions. I...guess I'm still in shock. I've wanted a child—children—for so long. Scott and I talked about having several and then, well, things didn't quite work out."

Though she didn't broadcast her past around, she had confided in Vicki after her first few weeks in Portland about the challenging years of her marriage and her husband's death.

"And the proud papa? What's his reaction?"

Tess closed her eyes, her stomach roiling just thinking about how on earth she would tell Quinn.

"I haven't told him yet. Actually, I...haven't talked to him in three months."

"If my math is right, this must be someone from Idaho since you've only been here for two months."

She sighed. "His foster mother was my last patient."

"Did you two have a big fight or something?"

She thought of all the accusations they had flung at each other that night. *You can't have what you want, your little fantasy happily-ever-after, and so kicking me out of your life completely is your version of throwing a pissy little temper tantrum.*

Now she was pregnant—*pregnant!*—and she didn't have the first idea what to do about it. She cringed, just imagining his reaction. He would probably accuse her of manipulating the entire thing as some Machiavellian plot to snare him into marriage.

Maybe you think if you push me out now, in a few weeks I'll come running back with tears and apologies, ready to give you anything you want. Even that all-important wedding ring that's apparently the only thing you think matters.

She pushed away the bitter memory, trying to drag her attention back to the problem at hand, this pregnancy that had completely knocked the pins out from under her.

She didn't even know how it had happened. Since hearing the news from her doctor, she had been wracking her brain about their time together and she could swear he used protection every single time. The only possibility was one time when they were in the shower and both became a little too carried away to think about the consequences.

She had been a nurse for ten years and she knew perfectly well that once was all it took but she never expected this to happen to her.

"You could say we had a fight," she finally answered Vicki. "We didn't part on exactly amiable terms."

"If you need to take a little time, I can cover your shift. Why don't you take the rest of the day off?"

"No. I'm okay. I just need a moment to collect my thoughts. I promise, I can put it out of my head and focus on my patients."

"At least take a quick break and go on out to the roof for some fresh air. I think the rain's finally stopped and it might help you clear your head."

She wanted to be tough and insist she was fine. But

the hard truth was she felt as if an atomic bomb had just been dropped in her life.

"Clearing my head would be good. Thanks."

When she rose, Vicki gathered her against her ample breast for a tight hug. "It will be okay, sweetheart. If this is what you want, I'm thrilled for you. I know if anyone can handle single motherhood, you can."

She had serious doubts right now about her ability to handle even the next five minutes, but she still appreciated the other woman's faith in her.

As she walked outside into the wet and cold January afternoon, she gazed out at the city sprawled out below her. So much for the best-laid plans. When she left Pine Gulch, she had been certain that she had everything figured out. Her life would be different but she had relished the excitement of making changes and facing new challenges.

In her wildest dreams, she never anticipated this particular challenge.

She pressed a hand to her abdomen, to the tiny life growing at a rapid pace there.

A child.

Quinn's child.

Emotions choked her throat, both joy and fear.

This pregnancy might not have been in her plans, but no matter what happened, she would love this child. She already did, even though she had only known of its existence for a short time.

She pressed her hand to her abdomen again. She had to tell Quinn. Even if he was bitter and angry and believed she had somehow manipulated circumstances to this end, she had to tell him. Withholding the knowledge of his child from him would be wrong, no matter how he reacted.

She only hoped she could somehow find the courage.

Two weeks later, she was still searching desperately for that strength. With each day that passed, it seemed more elusive than sunshine in a Portland winter.

Every morning since learning she was pregnant, she awoke with the full intention of calling him that day. But the hours slipped away and she made excuse after excuse to herself.

He was busy. She was working. She would wait until evening. She didn't have his number.

All of them were only pitiful justification for her to give in to her fears. That was the hard truth. She was afraid, pure and simple. Imagining his response kept her up at night and she was quite certain was contributing to the nausea she faced every morning.

That she continued to cater to that fear filled her with shame. She wasn't a weak woman and she hated that she was acting like it.

The night before, she had resolved that she couldn't put it off any longer. It was past time for her to act as the pregnancy seemed more real each day. Already, she was beginning to bump out and she was grateful her work scrubs had drawstring waists, since all her other slacks were starting to feel a little snug.

No more excuses. The next day was Saturday and she knew she had to tell him. Though she wanted nothing more than to take the coward's way out and communicate via phone—or, even better, e-mail—she had decided a man deserved to know he was going to become a father in person.

But figuring out how to find the man in Seattle was turning into more of a challenge than she expected.

She sat once more on the rooftop garden of the hospital on her lunch break, her cell phone in her hand as she punched in Easton Springhill's phone number as a last resort.

Easton's voice rose in surprise when she answered. "Tess! I was just thinking about you!"

"Oh?"

"I've been meaning to check in and see how life in the big city is treating you."

She gazed out through the gray mist at the buildings and neighborhoods that had become familiar friends to her during her frequent rooftop breaks. "Good. I like it here. I suppose Pine Gulch will always be home but I'm settling in."

"I'm so glad to hear that. You deserve some happiness."

And she would have it, she vowed. No matter what Quinn Southerland had to say about their child.

"How are you?" she stalled. "I mean really."

Easton was silent for a moment. "All right, I guess. I'm trying to stay busy. It's calving time so I'm on the run all the time, which I suppose is a blessing."

"I'm sorry I haven't called to check on you before now. I've thought of you often."

"No problem. You've been busy starting a new life. By the way," Easton went on, "I checked in on your morning coffee klatch crowd the other day and they all miss you like crazy. I never realized old Sal Martinez had such a thing for you."

She laughed, thinking of the dearly familiar old-timers who could always be counted on to lift her spirits. "What can I say? I'm pretty popular with eighty-year-old men who have cataracts."

Maybe she was making a mistake in her decision to stay in Portland and raise her baby. Moving back to Pine Gulch would give her child structure, community. Instant family. She had time to make that particular decision, she told herself. First things first.

"Listen, I'm sorry to bother you but I'm trying to reach Quinn and I can't find his personal contact information."

"You can't?" Easton's shock filtered clearly through the phone and Tess winced. She had never told her friend that she and Quinn had parted on difficult terms. She supposed she had assumed Quinn would have told her.

"No. I tried to call his company and ended up having to go through various gatekeepers who weren't inclined to be cooperative."

"He can be harder to reach than the Oval Office sometimes. I've got his cell number programmed on mine so I don't have it memorized but hang on while I look it up."

She returned in a moment and recited the number and Tess scribbled it down.

"Can you tell me his home address?" she said, feeling awkward and uncomfortable that she had to ask.

Easton paused for a long moment. "Is something wrong, Tess?"

If you only knew the half of it, she thought.

"Not at all," she lied. "I just… I wanted to mail him something," she improvised quickly.

She could tell her friend didn't quite buy her explanation but to her vast relief, Easton recited the address.

"You'll have to find the zip code. I don't know that off the top of my head."

"I can look it up. Thanks."

"Are you sure nothing's wrong? You sound distracted."

"Just busy. Listen, I'm on a break at the hospital and really need to get back to my patients. It was great talking to you. I'll call you next week sometime when we both have more time to chat."

"You do that."

They said their goodbyes, though she could still hear the questions in Easton's voice. She was happy to hang up the phone. Another moment and she would be blurting it all out. Easton was too darned perceptive and Tess had always been a lousy liar.

She certainly couldn't tell Easton about her pregnancy until she'd had a chance to share the news with Quinn first.

She gazed at the address in her hand, her stomach tangled in knots at the encounter that loomed just over the horizon.

Whatever happened, her baby would still have her.

Talk about acting on the spur of the moment.

Quinn cruised down the winding, thickly forested street in Portland, wondering what the hell he was doing there.

He wasn't one for spontaneity and impulsive acts of insanity, but here he was, trying to follow his GPS directions through an unfamiliar neighborhood in the dark and the rain.

She might not even be home. For all he knew, she could be working nights or even, heaven forbid, on a date.

At the thought, he was tempted to just turn his car

around and drive back to Seattle. He was crazy to just show up at her place out of the blue like this. But then, when it came to Tess and his behavior toward her, sanity hadn't exactly been in plentiful supply.

He felt edgy and off balance, as if he didn't even know himself anymore and the man he always thought he'd been. He was supposed to be a careful business-man, known for his forethought and savvy strategizing.

He certainly *wasn't* a man who drove a hundred and fifty miles on a whim, all because of a simple phone call from Easton.

When she called him he had just been wrapping up an important meeting. The moment she said Tess had called her looking for his address and phone number, his brain turned to mush and he hadn't been able to focus on anything else. Not the other executives still in the room with him or the contract Southerland Shipping had just signed or the route reconfiguration they were negotiating.

All he could think about was Tess.

His conversation with Easton played through his mind now as he followed the GPS directions.

"Something seemed off, you know?" she had said. "I couldn't put my finger on it but she sounded upset. I just wanted to give you a heads-up that she might be trying to reach you."

As it had then, his mind raced in a hundred different directions. What could be wrong? After three months of empty, deafening silence between them, why was she suddenly trying to make contact?

He only had the patience to wait an hour for her call before he couldn't stand the uncertainty another moment.

In that instant, as he made the call to excuse himself

from a fundraiser he'd been obligated to attend for the evening, he had realized with stark clarity how very self-deceptive he had been for the past three months.

He had spent twelve weeks trying to convince himself he was over Tess Claybourne, that their brief relationship had been a mistake but one that he was quite certain had left no lasting scars on his heart.

The moment he heard her name, a wild rush of emotion had surged through him, like water gushing from a dam break, and he realized just how much effort it had taken him to shove everything back to the edges of his subconscious.

Only in his dreams did he let himself remember those magical days he and Tess had shared, the peace and comfort he found in her arms.

He had definitely been fooling himself. Their time together had had a profound impact on his world. Since then, he found himself looking at everything from a different perspective. All the things he used to find so fulfilling—his business pursuits, his fundraising engagements, boating on the Sound—now seemed colorless and dull. Tedious, even.

Southerland was expanding at a rapid pace and he should have been thrilled to watch this company he had created begin at last to attain some of the goals he had set for it. Instead, he found himself most evenings sitting on his deck on Mercer Island, staring out at the lights reflecting on the water and wondering why all the successes felt so empty.

No doubt some of the funk he seemed to have slipped into was due to the grieving process he was still undergoing for Jo.

But he had a somber suspicion that a large portion of that emptiness inside him was due to Tess and the hole she had carved out in his life.

He sighed. Might as well be completely frank—with himself, at least. Tess hadn't done any carving. He had been the one wielding the butcher knife by pushing her away the first chance he had.

He couldn't blame her for that last ugly scene between them. At least not completely. At the first obstacle in their growing relationship, he had jumped on the defensive and had been far too quick to shove her away.

In his business life, he tried to focus most on the future by positioning his company to take advantage of market trends and growth areas. He didn't like looking back, except to examine his mistakes in an effort to figure out what he could fix.

And he had made plenty of mistakes where Tess was concerned. As he examined what had happened three months earlier in Pine Gulch, he had to admit that he had been scared, pure and simple.

He needed to see her again. He owed her an apology, a proper goodbye without the anger and unfounded accusations he had hurled at her.

That's why he was here, trying to find her house in the pale, watery moonlight.

His GPS announced her address a moment later and he pulled into the driveway of a small pale rose brick house, a strange mix of dread and anticipation twisting around his gut as he gazed through the rain-splattered windshield.

Her house reminded him very much of the one in Pine Gulch on a slightly smaller scale. Both were older homes with established trees and gardens. The white shutters and gable gave it a charming seaside cottage appeal. It was surrounded by shrubs and what looked like an extensive flower garden, bare now except for a few clumps of dead growth.

He imagined that in the springtime, it would explode with color but just now, in early February, it only looked cold and barren in the rain.

He refused to think about how he could use that same metaphor for his life the past three months.

Smoke curled from the chimney and lights gleamed from several windows. As he parked in the driveway, he thought he saw a shadow move past the window inside and his breathing quickened.

For one cowardly moment, he was tempted again to put the car in Reverse and head back to Seattle. Maybe Easton had her signals crossed and Tess wasn't really looking for him. Maybe she only wanted his address to send him a kiss-off letter telling him how happy she was without him.

Even if that was the case, he had come this far. He couldn't back out now.

The rain had slowed to a cold mist as he walked up the curving sidewalk to her front door. He rang the doorbell, his insides a corkscrew of nerves.

A moment later, the door opened and the weeks and distance and pain between them seemed to fall away.

She looked fresh and bright, her loose auburn curls framing those lovely features that wore an expectant look—for perhaps half a second, anyway, until she registered who was at her doorstep.

"Quinn!" she gasped, the color leaching from her face like old photographs left in the desert.

"Hello, Tess."

She said nothing, just continued to stare at him for a good thirty seconds. He couldn't tell if she was aghast to find him on her doorstep or merely surprised.

Wishing he had never given in to this crazy impulse to drive two and a half hours, he finally spoke. "May I come in?"

She gazed at him for another long moment. When he was certain she would slam the door in his face, she held it open farther and stepped back so he had room to get through. "I… Yes. Of course."

He followed her inside and had a quick impression of a warm space dominated by a pale rose brick fireplace, blazing away against the rainy night. The living room looked comfortable and bright, with plump furniture and colorful pillows and her upright piano in one corner, still covered with photographs.

"Can I get you something to drink?" she asked. "I'll confess, I don't have many options but I do have some wine I was given as a housewarming gift when I moved here."

"I'm fine. Thanks."

The silence stretched out between them, taut and awkward. He had a sudden vivid memory of lying in her bed with her, bodies entwined as they talked for hours.

His chest ached suddenly with a deep hunger to taste that closeness again.

"You're pale," he said, thrusting his hands in the pockets of his jacket and curling them into fists where she couldn't see. "Are you ill? Easton said you called her and she was worried."

She frowned slightly, as if still trying to make sense

of his sudden appearance. "You're here because Easton asked you to check on me?"

For a moment, he thought about answering yes. That would be the easy out for both of them, but he couldn't do it.

Though he had suspected it, he suddenly knew with relentless clarity that *she* was the reason for the emptiness of the past three months.

He had never felt so very solitary as he had without Tess in his world to share his accomplishments and his worries. To laugh with, to maybe cry with. To share hopes for the future and help him heal from the past.

He wanted all those things she had talked about, exactly what she had created for herself here.

He wanted a home. He wanted to live in a house with carefully tended gardens that burst with color in the springtime, a place that provided a warm haven against the elements on a bitter winter night.

And he wanted to share that with Tess.

He wanted love.

Like a junkie jonesing for his next fix, he craved the peace he had found only with Tess.

"No," he finally admitted hoarsely. "I'm here because I missed you."

Chapter Sixteen

She stared at him, her eyes wide and the same color as a storm-tossed sea. "You…what?"

He sighed, cursing the unruly slip of his tongue. "Forget I said that. Yeah, I'm here because Easton asked me to check on you."

"You're lying." Though the words alone might have sounded arrogant, he saw the vulnerability in her eyes and something else, something that almost looked like a tiny flicker of hope.

He gazed at her, his blood pulsing loudly in his ears. He had come this far. He might as well take a step further, until he was completely out on the proverbial limb hanging over the bottomless crevasse.

"All right. Yes. I missed you. Are you happy now?"

She was quiet for a long moment, the only sound in the house the quiet murmuring of the fire.

"No," she finally whispered. "Not at all. I've been so miserable, Quinn."

Her voice sounded small and watery and completely genuine. He gave a low groan and couldn't take this distance between them another second. He yanked his hands out of his pockets and reached for her and she wrapped her arms fiercely around his neck, holding on for dear life.

Emotions choked in his throat and he buried his face in the crook of her shoulder.

Here. This was what he had missed. Having her in his arms again was like coming home, like heaven, like everything good he had ever been afraid to wish for.

How had he ever been stupid enough to push away the best thing that had ever happened to him?

He kissed her and a wild flood of emotions welled up in his throat at the intense sweetness of having her in his arms once more.

"I'm sorry," he murmured against her mouth. "So damn sorry. I've been a pathetic wreck for three lousy months."

"I have, too," she said. "You ruined *everything*."

He gave a short, rough laugh. "Did I?"

"I had this great new job, this new life I was trying to create for myself. It was supposed to be so perfect. Instead, I've been completely desolate. All I've been able to think about is you and how much I…" Her voice trailed off and he caught his breath, waiting for her to finish the sentence.

"How much you what?" he said when she remained stubbornly silent.

"How much I missed you," she answered and he was aware of a flicker of disappointment thrumming through him as he sensed that wasn't what she had intended to say at all.

He kissed her again and she sighed against his mouth, her arms tight around him.

Despite the cold February rain, he felt as if spring was finally blooming in his heart.

"Everything you said to me that last night was exactly right, Tess. I've given the past too much power in my life."

"Oh, Quinn. I had no right to say those things to you. I've been sorry every since."

He shook his head. "You were right."

"Everyone handles their pain differently. The only thing I know is that everyone has some in his or her life. It's as inevitable as…as breathing and dying."

"Well, you taught me I didn't have to let it control everything I do. Look at you. Your dreams of a happily-ever-after came crashing down around you with Scott's accident. But you didn't become bitter or angry at the world."

"I had my moments of despair, believe me."

His chest ached for her all over again and he cringed at the memory of how he had lashed out at her their last night together in Pine Gulch, accusing her of being the same spoiled girl he had known in high school.

He hadn't meant any of those ugly words. Even as he had said them, he had known she was a far different woman.

He had been in love with her that night, had been probably since that first moment she had sat beside him on the floor of her spare room and listened to him pour out all the ugly memories he kept carefully bottled up inside.

No. Earlier, he admitted.

He had probably been a little in love with her in high school, when he had thought he hated her. He had just been too afraid to admit the truth to himself.

"But despite everything you went through, you didn't let your trials destroy you or make you cynical or hard," he said gently, holding her close. "You still open your heart so easily. It's one of the things I love the most about you."

Tess stared at him, her heart pulsing a crazy rhythm in her chest. He couldn't have just said what she thought he did. Quinn didn't believe in love. But the echo of his words resounded in her head.

Still, she needed a little confirmation that she wasn't completely hearing things.

"You…what?"

His mouth quirked into that half grin she had adored since junior high school.

"You're going to make me say it, aren't you? All right. That's one of the millions of things I love about you. Right up there at the top of the list is your big, generous, unbreakable heart."

"Not unbreakable," she corrected, still not daring to believe his words. "It has felt pretty shattered the past three months."

He let out a sound of regret just before he kissed her again, his mouth warm and gentle. At the devastating tenderness in his kiss, emotions rose in her throat and her eyes felt scratchy with unshed tears.

"I'm sorry," he murmured between kisses. "So damn sorry. Can you forgive me? I've been a stupid, scared idiot."

He paused, his eyes intense. "You have to cut me a little slack, though."

"Do I?"

Her arch tone drew a smile. "It's only fair. I'm a man who's never been in love before. If you want the truth, it scares the hell out of me."

I'm a man who's never been in love before.

The words soaked through all the pain and loneliness and fear of the past three months.

He loved her. This wasn't some crazy dream where she would wake up once more with a tear-soaked pillow wrapped in her arms. Quinn was standing here in her living room, holding her tightly and saying things she never would have believed if she didn't feel the strength of his arms around her.

He loved her.

She pulled his mouth to hers and kissed him hard, pouring all the heat and joy and wonder spinning around inside her into her kiss. When she at last drew away, they were both breathing raggedly and his eyes looked dazed.

"I love you, Quinn. I love you so much. I wanted to make a new life for myself here in Portland, a new start. But all I've been able to think about is how much I miss you."

"Tess—" He groaned her name and leaned down to kiss her again but she gathered what tiny spark of strength remained and stepped slightly away from him, desperate for a little space to gather her thoughts.

"I love you. But I have to tell you something…"

"Me first." He squeezed her fingers. "I know you think we want two different things out of life. I'll admit, it would probably be a bit of a stretch to say I've had some sudden miraculous change of heart and I'm now completely ready to rush right off to find a wedding chapel."

Well, that would certainly make what she had to tell him a little more difficult. Some of her apprehension must have showed in her eyes because he brought their clasped fingers to his mouth and pressed a kiss to the back of her hand.

"But the thought of being without you scares me a hell of a lot more than the idea of hearts and flowers and wedding cake. I want everything with you. I know I can get there with your help. It just might take me a few months."

"We have a few months."

"I hope we have a lot longer than that. I want forever, Tess."

She gazed at him, dark and gorgeous and male, with clear sincerity in his stunning eyes. He meant what he said. He wasn't going use his past as an excuse anymore.

She couldn't quite adjust to this sudden shift. Only an hour ago, she had been sitting at her solitary dining table with a TV dinner in front of her, lonely and achy and frightened at the prospect of having to face his reaction the next day to the news of the child they had created together.

And here he was using words like *forever* with her.

She still hadn't told him the truth, she reminded herself. Everything might change with a few simple words. And though she wanted to hang on to this lovely feeling for the rest of her life, she knew she had to tell him.

Though it was piercingly difficult, she pulled her hands away from his and crossed her arms in front of her.

"I need to tell you something first. It may…change your perspective."

He looked confused and even a little apprehensive, as if bracing himself for bad news. "What's wrong?"

"Nothing. At least I don't think so. I hope you don't, either."

She twisted her fingers together, trying to gather her nerves.

"Tell me," he said after a long pause.

With a deep breath, she plunged forward. "I don't know how this happened. Well, I know how it happened. I'm a nurse, after all. But not *how* it happened, if you know what I mean. I mean, we took precautions but even the best precautions sometimes fail…" Her voice trailed off.

"Tess. Just tell me."

"I'm pregnant."

The words hung between them, heavy, dense. He said nothing for a long time, just continued to stare at her.

She searched his gaze but she couldn't read anything in his expression. Was he happy, terrified, angry? She didn't have the first idea.

She pressed her lips together. "I know. I was shocked, too. I only found out a few weeks ago and I've been trying to figure out how to tell you. That's why I called Easton for your address. I was going to drive to Seattle tomorrow. I've been so scared."

That evoked a reaction from him—surprise.

"Scared? Why?"

She sighed. "I didn't want you to think it was all part

of some grand, manipulative plan. I swear, I didn't expect this, Quinn. You have to believe me. We were careful. I know we were. The only thing I can think is that…that time in the shower, remember?"

Something flickered across his features then, something that sent heat scorching through her.

"I remember," he said, his voice gruff.

He didn't say anything more and after a moment, she wrapped her arms more tightly around herself, cold suddenly despite the fire blazing merrily in her hearth.

"I know this changes everything. You said yourself you're not ready quite yet for all of that. I completely understand. I don't want you to feel pressured, Quinn. But I…I love her already. The baby and I will be fine on our own if you decide you're not ready. I'll wait as long as it takes. I have savings. I won't ask anything of you, I swear."

Again, something sparked in his gaze. "I thought you said you love me."

"I did. I do."

"Then how can you think I would possibly walk away now?"

His eyes glittered with a fierce emotion that suddenly took her breath away. Hope began to pulse through her and she curled her fingers into her fists, afraid to let it explode inside her.

"A baby." He breathed out the word like a prayer or a curse, she couldn't quite tell. "When?"

"Sometime in early July."

"An Independence Day baby. We can name her Liberty."

Her laugh was a half sob and she reached blindly for

him. He swept her into his arms and pulled her close as that joy burst out like fireworks in the Pine Gulch night sky.

"Liberty Jo," she insisted.

His eyes softened and he kissed her with more of that heart-shaking tenderness. "A baby," he murmured after a long while. His eyes were dazed as he placed a hand over her tiny bump and she covered his hand with hers.

"You're not upset?" she asked.

"*Numb* is a better word. But underneath the shock is…joy. I don't know how to explain it but it feels right."

"Oh, Quinn. That was my reaction, too. I was scared to death to find out I was pregnant. But the idea of a child—*your* child—filled me with so much happiness and peace. That's a perfect word. It feels *right*."

"I love you, Tess." He pressed his mouth to hers again. "You took a man who was hard and cynical, who tried to convince himself he was happy being alone, and showed him everything good and right that was missing in his world."

He pressed his mouth to hers and in his kiss she tasted joy and healing and the promise of a brilliant future.

* * * * *

**We'll be spotlighting a different series
every month throughout 2009
to celebrate our 60th anniversary.**

Look for Silhouette® Nocturne™ in October!

Travel through time to experience tales
that reach the boundaries of life and death.
Bestselling authors Lindsay McKenna, Cindy
Dees, P.C. Cast and Merline Lovelace join
together in a brand-new, four-book
Time Raiders miniseries.

TIME RAIDERS

August—*The Seeker*
by *USA TODAY* bestselling author Lindsay McKenna

September—*The Slayer* by Cindy Dees

October—*The Avenger*
by *New York Times* bestselling author and
coauthor of the House of Night novels P.C. Cast

November—*The Protector*
by *USA TODAY* bestselling author Merline Lovelace

Available wherever books are sold.